D0527886

EGMONT

We bring stories to life

First published in Great Britain 2018 by Egmont Books UK Limited
2 Minster Court, 10th Floor, London EC3R 7BB

Illustrations by Gregory Sokol
Written by Dr. Gareth Moore
Designed by Richie Hull

ISBN 978 1 4052 8888 0
68010/006
Printed in UK

To find more great *Star Wars* books, visit
www.egmontbooks.co.uk/starwars

STAR WARS™

YODA'S PUZZLES

Hmmm?
Ah. Found me, you have. The first test, you have passed.
Come closer, now. Yes, do not be afraid. Your training – completed, it must be.
The path of the Jedi requires wisdom, hmm? A lightsaber is sharp, but sharper must be your wits. A Jedi must be strong and nimble, yes – but only as strong and nimble as your mind, will you be.
These puzzles, then – solve them, you must. Walk the path from Padawan to Knight, to Master. Patience you must have; only with time and deep thought can these secrets be unlocked...
May the Force be with you!
– Master Yoda

Who's Who?

DIFFICULTY:

Can you find all of the characters hidden in this word search grid? Their names can be written either forwards or backwards, and in any direction – including diagonally. Ignore any spaces or dashes when looking for the names.

L	E	N	J	M	A	C	E	W	I	N	D	U	U	S	G
U	A	K	A	Q	U	I	G	O	N	J	I	N	N	P	L
Y	N	N	O	D	C	I	E	A	D	M	T	E	W	A	U
L	A	O	D	B	M	H	N	D	A	R	Y	R	T	D	K
U	K	R	A	O	I	I	E	U	K	T	N	O	T	M	E
A	I	E	R	D	C	W	R	W	A	A	N	L	U	E	S
M	N	M	T	D	O	A	A	A	B	C	E	Y	H	A	K
H	S	A	H	D	U	Y	L	N	L	A	Y	K	E	M	Y
T	K	D	V	H	N	U	G	R	K	A	C	E	H	I	W
R	Y	E	A	A	T	N	R	S	I	E	C	C	T	D	A
A	W	O	D	N	D	E	I	A	W	S	N	K	A	A	L
D	A	P	E	S	O	R	E	F	O	M	S	O	B	L	K
O	L	N	R	O	O	L	V	R	A	W	N	I	B	A	E
H	K	N	Y	L	K	A	O	M	E	N	A	I	A	I	R
N	E	E	U	O	U	D	U	O	L	R	A	L	J	N	S
P	R	I	N	C	E	S	S	L	E	I	A	A	O	N	S

Admiral Ackbar
Anakin Skywalker
Chewbacca
Count Dooku
Darth Maul
Darth Vader
Finn

General Grievous
Han Solo
Jabba The Hutt
Kylo Ren
Lando Calrissian
Luke Skywalker
Mace Windu

Obi-Wan Kenobi
Padmé Amidala
Poe Dameron
Princess Leia
Qui-Gon Jinn
Rey
Yoda

Binary Baffler

DIFFICULTY:

Luke Skywalker needs to fix a battered old astromech. The binary start-up sequence is incomplete – can you help him fill in the blanks to get the droid working again?

- Place three '0's and three '1's into each row and column
- There cannot be more than two '0's or two '1s' in sequence in any row or column

				1	1
0		0		1	0
1	1		1		0
1	1				

Transmission Impossible

DIFFICULTY: 

K-2SO is an Imperial droid that has been reprogrammed by Cassian. He is monitoring Imperial transmissions at their signal tower on the planet Scarif.

Can you work out the values transmitted by each tower?

To find the values, start with the number at the bottom of each tower and then follow the arrows to apply each step in turn. For example, in the first tower you should start with 7, then multiply by 10, then add 10, and so on. Try to work out the result of each tower in your head without making any written notes – just like a droid!

RESULT	RESULT	RESULT	RESULT
+20	×3	÷6	+20
÷3	+6	+6	÷4
-11	÷4	×2	×12
+10	×11	-10	÷2
×10	÷7	+17	-6
7	**28**	**14**	**14**

Traffic Jam

DIFFICULTY: 

Speeders criss-cross the skies of Coruscant, zipping from tower to tower. Can you help Obi-Wan and Anakin reach their destinations? Draw a path between each pair of identical numbers, using only horizontal and vertical lines. To avoid dangerous crashes, the paths cannot cross each other, and only one path can enter any square. Here's an example solution to show how it works:

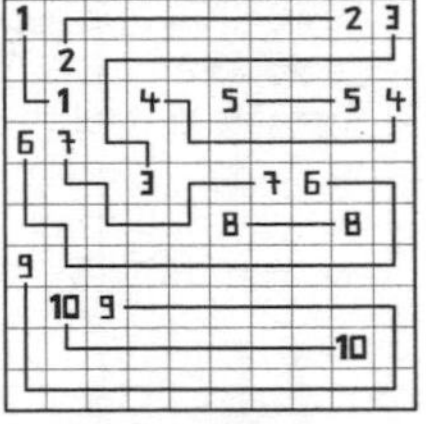

							1		2
1				3					4
2	3					5			
			6				6		
7	5								
		8					9		
				4					10
			10						
	8							9	7

Boushh Bewildered

DIFFICULTY: 

Bounty hunter Boushh has forgotten an important password. Can you help work out what it could be?

Find the nine-letter password in the grid below. In addition, see how many more words of three or more letters you can spell!

To spell a word, start on any letter and then trace a path up/down/left/right from letter to neighbouring letter, but without visiting any square more than once within a word. For example, you could start on the 'R' on the right-hand side, move up to 'A', and left to 'T' to spell 'RAT'. Diagonal moves are not allowed.

T	T	A
H	S	R
G	I	L

Puzzle Protocol

DIFFICULTY:

It's time to upgrade C-3PO's translation software – seven million languages just isn't enough any more! Which of the possible circuit boards, 1 to 4, fits into the gap to complete his new circuitry?

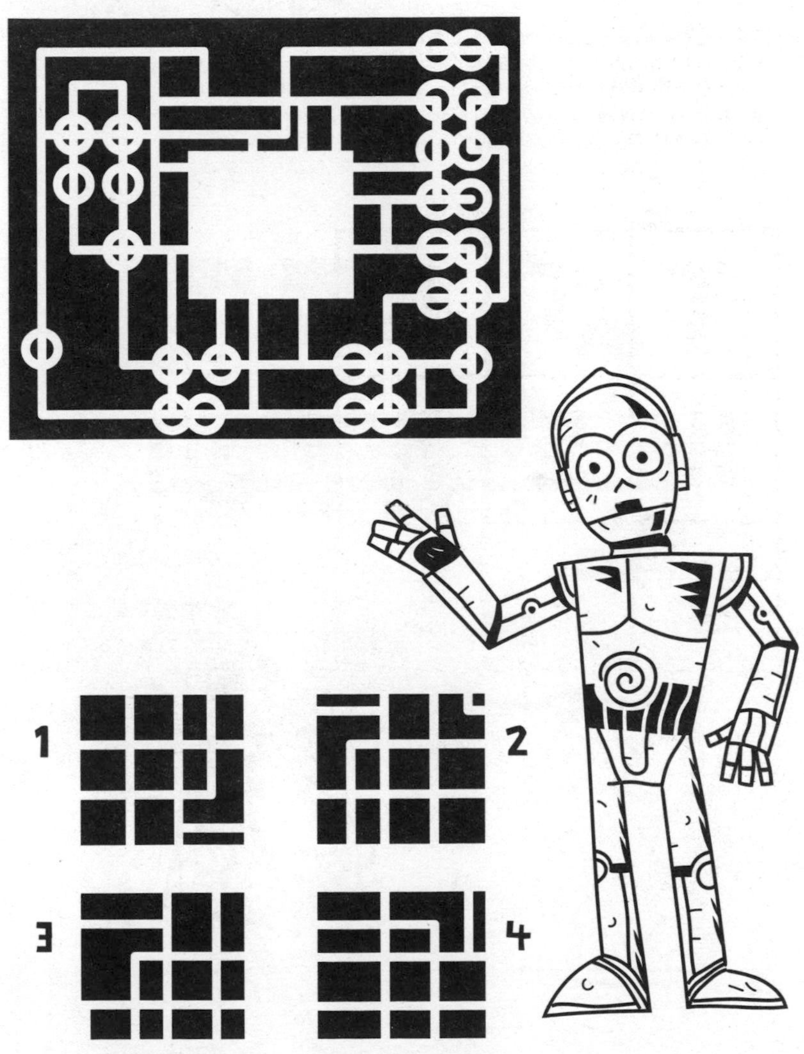

Greedy Greedo

DIFFICULTY: 

Greedo is breaking into a vault for his boss Jabba, but it has an unusual combination lock. Each dial can show one of three letters. At the moment, it spells 'STAND', but by changing the letter each dial is set to it can spell various different words.

To gain access to the vault he must spell out the words which solve the following clues. Can you work out all of the words?

1. Break the rules
2. A strong metal
3. Large or impressive
4. Desire for wealth
5. Take without asking
6. Shouted out

Dial 1	Dial 2	Dial 3	Dial 4	Dial 5
		I	A	L
C		E	E	T
S	T	A	N	D
G	R			
	H			

Corridor Code

DIFFICULTY:

A clue to the identity of a key member of the Rebellion is hidden within the corridors of this maze. Find your way from the entrance at the top all the way to the exit at the bottom, collecting letters as you go. Those letters that are directly on the exit route will spell out the name of the hidden person.

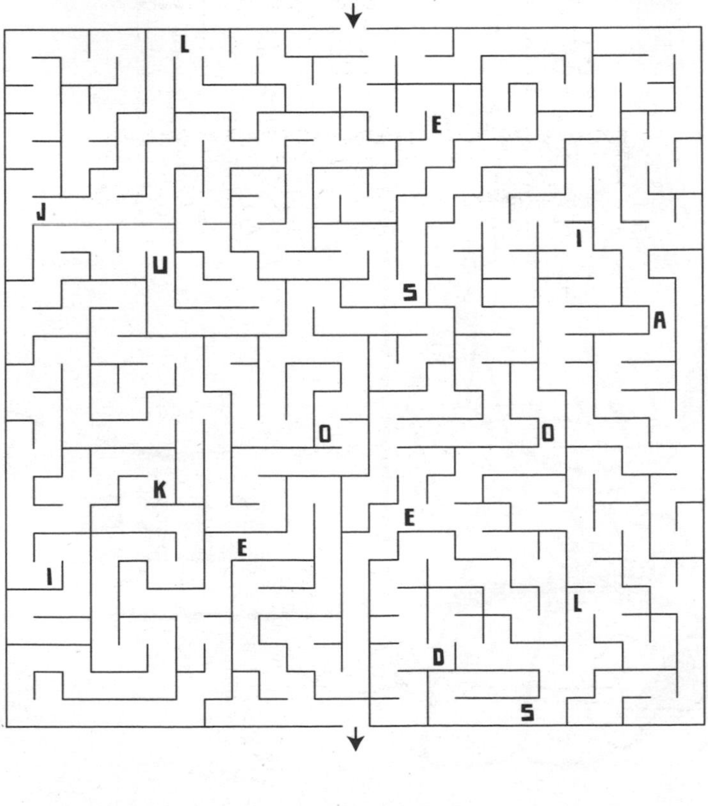

Mind Connection

DIFFICULTY:

Qui-Gon will help you learn to see with the Force, by changing 'MIND' into 'SEES' in just four steps. At each step you should change just one letter to make a new word, without rearranging any of the letters. For example, you *could* start by changing MIND to MINE (though that will lead you down the wrong path . . .)

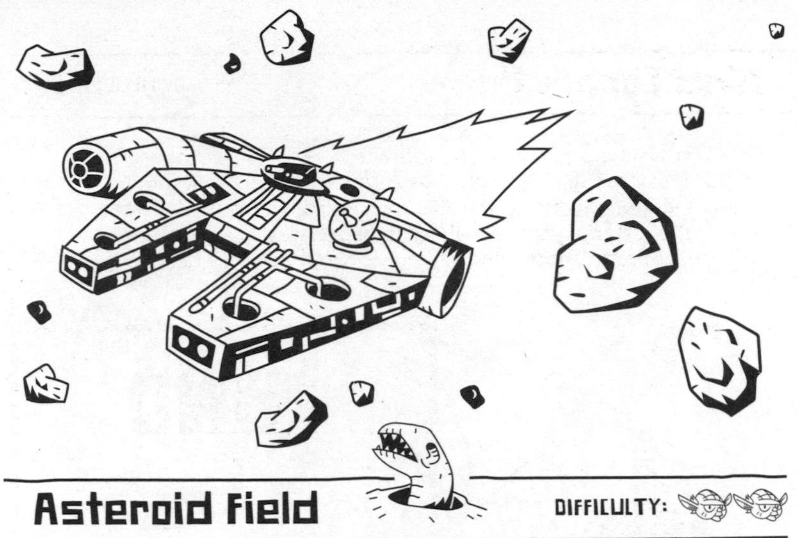

Asteroid Field

DIFFICULTY:

The *Millennium Falcon*'s scanner dish has taken a hit from an asteroid, and the navicomputer is malfunctioning! You can't see the rest of the asteroids in your path. All you know is that some of the empty squares in the scanner grid below conceal an asteroid, and that the numbers tell you how many of their touching squares – including diagonally touching squares – contain an asteroid. None of the numbered squares have an asteroid in, and no square can contain more than one. Can you find all of the asteroids before it's too late?

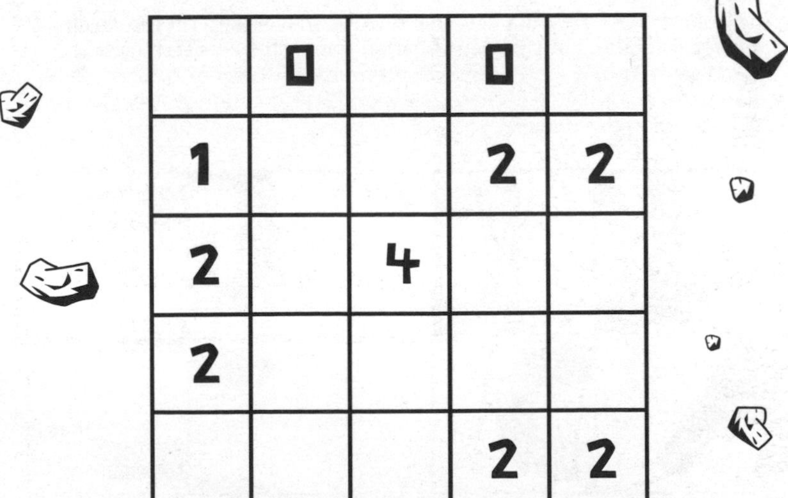

	0		0	
1			2	2
2		4		
2				
			2	2

Jawa Junk

DIFFICULTY:

The Jawas have found a new droid while scavenging on the desert planet Tatooine, but the identification panels have been mixed up. Each set of four panels has been rearranged – but not rotated. Can you work out what two-character identification code was originally displayed on the panels?

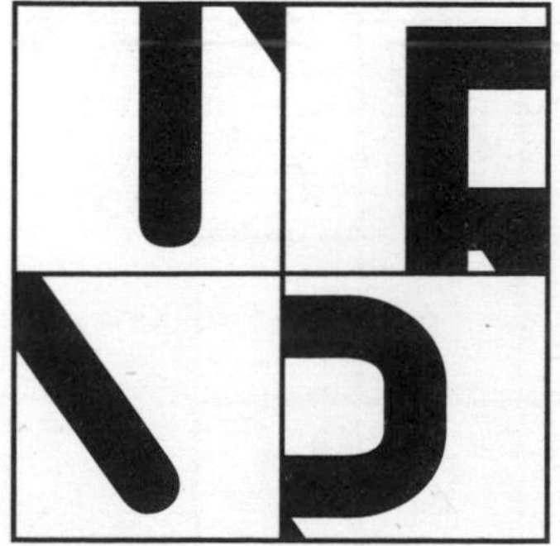

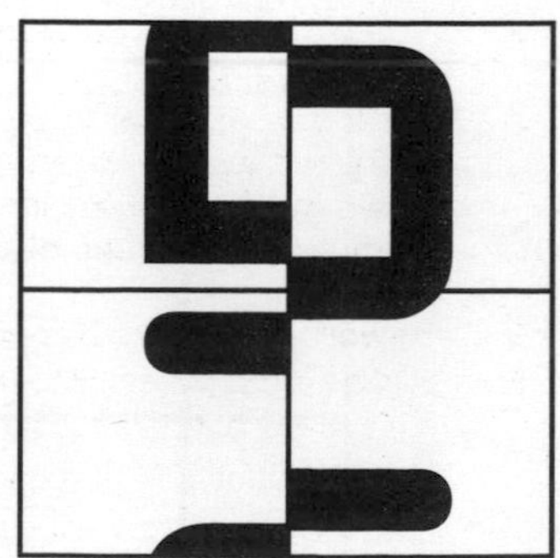

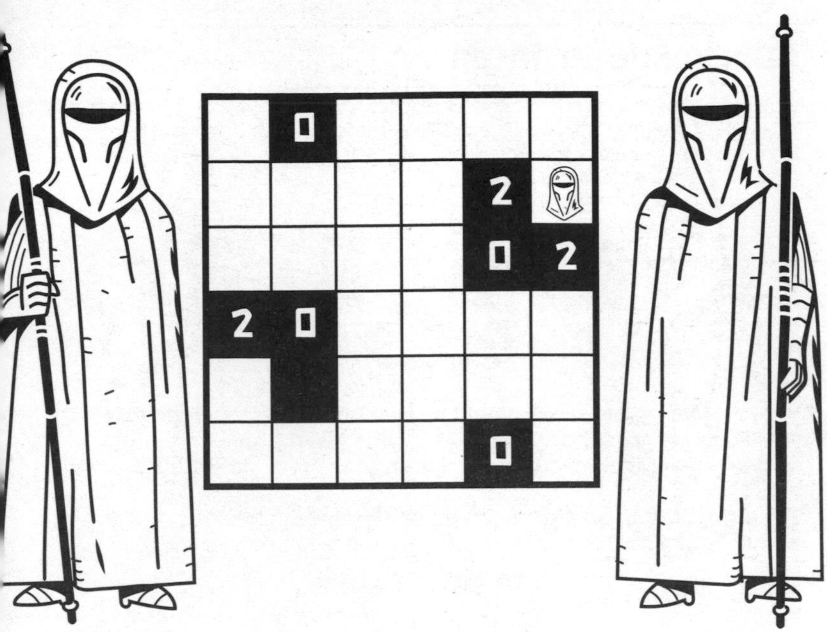

Guards, Guards!

DIFFICULTY:

The Emperor has commanded you to assign elite guards to his palace. Place eight guards in the grid above, following these rules:

- You can only place guards in empty squares, not the shaded squares, and only one in each square.
- Numbers in the shaded squares tell you how many guards you need to place in the squares immediately to the left, right, above or below.
- Guards can see all the way left, right, up and down from their square, but not through shaded squares.
- No two guards can see each other.
- All empty squares can be seen by at least one guard.

Can you work out where all eight of the guards should go? One has been placed for you to start you off.

Cargo Conundrum

DIFFICULTY: 

Chewbacca needs to load five rebel transports with important cargo. There are six types of package, with weights as shown:

Which types of packages should he load onto each freighter, given the target weights shown below? He can't use the same type of package more than once on a single ship.

For example, to load a total weight of 31 he would load the 4, 7, 9 and 11 weight packages, since 4 + 7 + 9 + 11 = 31.

Ship 1: Total weight = 15
Ship 2: Total weight = 22
Ship 3: Total weight = 26
Ship 4: Total weight = 29
Ship 5: Total weight = 34

Sign Language

DIFFICULTY: 

All of the signs in the Imperial bunker on Endor have been encrypted in order to confuse the enemy. By shading in some of the squares in the image below, can you work out which direction the rebels should head next?

Numbers at the start of a row or column indicate the number of shaded squares in that row or column. All shaded squares within a row or column touch each other in a continuous line, without any unshaded squares between them. One column has been done, to get you started!

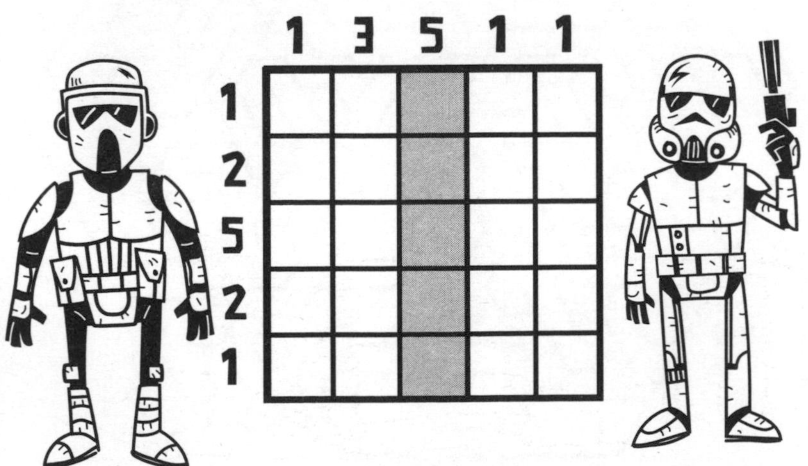

Rebel Run

DIFFICULTY:

Jyn is running from Imperial troops! Can you lose them in this maze of streets? Guide her from the inwards-facing arrow at the top to the exit arrow at the bottom as quickly as you can.

Tarkin's Teaser

DIFFICULTY: 

Grand Moff Tarkin has intercepted rebel code sequences. Crack their cypher by completing each of the following numerical sequences. In each case there is a mathematical connection between each number and its preceding number, or numbers. Can you help Tarkin work out what comes next in each sequence? The first has been done for you - each number is 4 more than the one before.

1)	3	7	11	15	19	23	27
2)	1	2	4	8	16	32	___
3)	2	4	7	11	16	22	___
4)	3	4	7	11	18	29	___
5)	192	96	48	24	12	6	___

Hungry Hungry Hutt

DIFFICULTY: 

Jabba's chef is running out of ingredients, and his boss is hungry! There are two separate piles of ready-to-eat Klatooine Paddy Frogs, and you know that each started off as a 5x3x3 stack of crates as shown below.

How many frog crates remain in each of the two piles below? None of the crates are 'floating', so if you can see one at the top of a column on the second or third layer then you know there must be one or two beneath, as appropriate.

ORIGINAL PILE

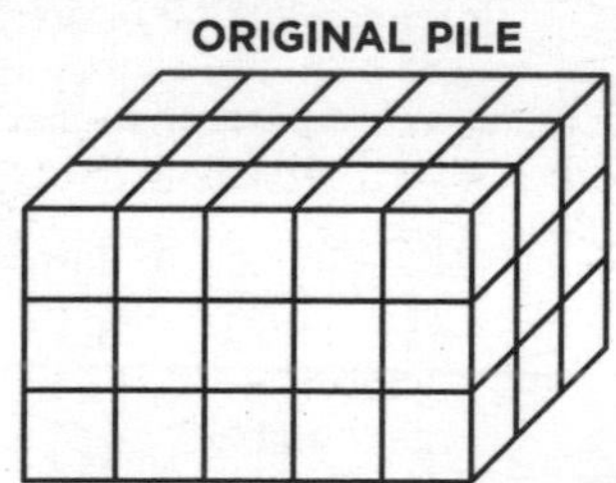

PILE 1

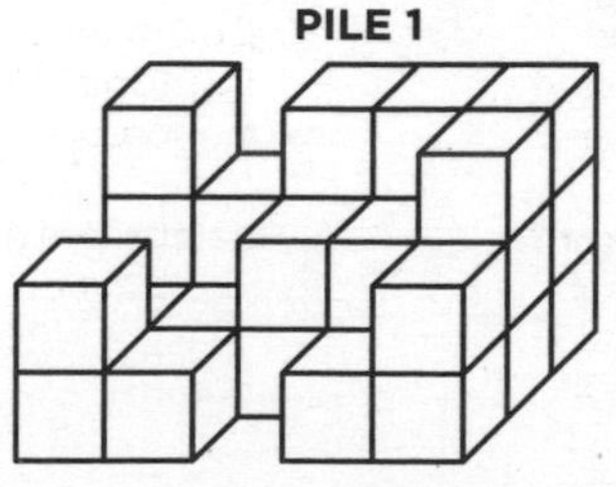

PILE 2

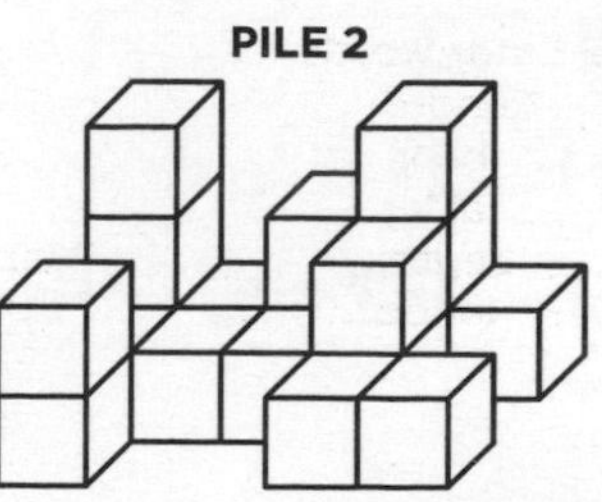

Star Tours

DIFFICULTY:

Pilot droid RX-24 has forgotten the stops on his tour! Can you help him remember? Place all of the planets and moons into the grid, once each, so that they read either across or down with one letter per box. Ignore any spaces in the planet and moon names when fitting them in.

4 letter words
Eadu
Teth

5 letter words
Endor
Ibaar
Jakku
Jedha
Naboo

6 letter words
Agamar
Bespin
Carlac
Kessel
Rugosa
Zanbar

7 letter words
Dagobah
Mon Cala
Onderon

8 letter word
Alderaan

9 letter words
Coruscant
Dantooine
Mandalore

10 letter word
Skako Minor

Lightsaber Lesson

DIFFICULTY: 

The lightsaber: an elegant weapon for a more civilized time. Luke must learn to use it with precision and intelligence. As a test, he must cut the piece of material shown below into four pieces, cutting only along the grid lines. Each piece must be identical in shape, although they may appear rotated relative to one another - but not reflected. All of the material must be used, without any bits left over. Can you work out where to cut?

Hint: there are 16 squares in the shape, so each piece must consist of exactly 4 squares.

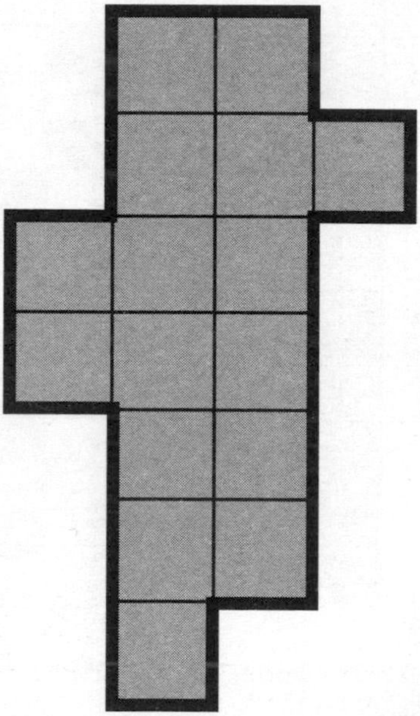

Ship Shape

DIFFICULTY:

Secret intelligence has reached the rebels, identifying the location of five enemy ships. Locate one cruiser, two fighters and two shuttles using just the information on the map below.

The rebels know that the ships are lying horizontally or vertically on the map, and each covers the number of squares shown by the key below. Squares with ships in don't touch each other - not even diagonally.

Numbers outside the grid reveal how many ship segments are contained in each row and column, as in the example.

Example:

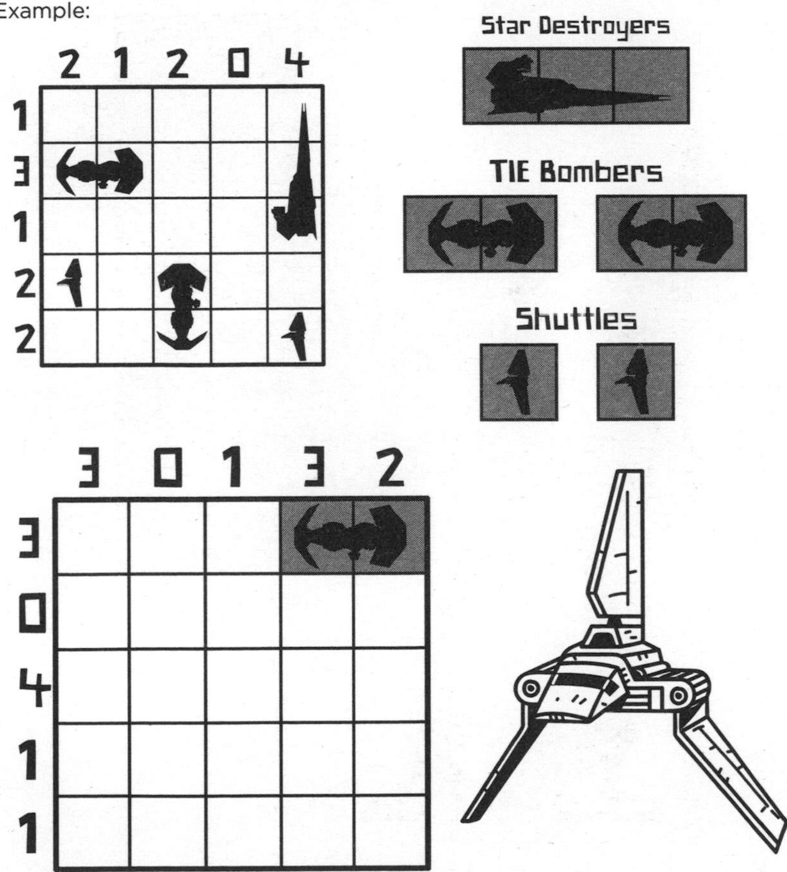

Mystery Master

DIFFICULTY: 

Join the numbered dots in numerical order from 1 to 115 to reveal a well-known Jedi Master.

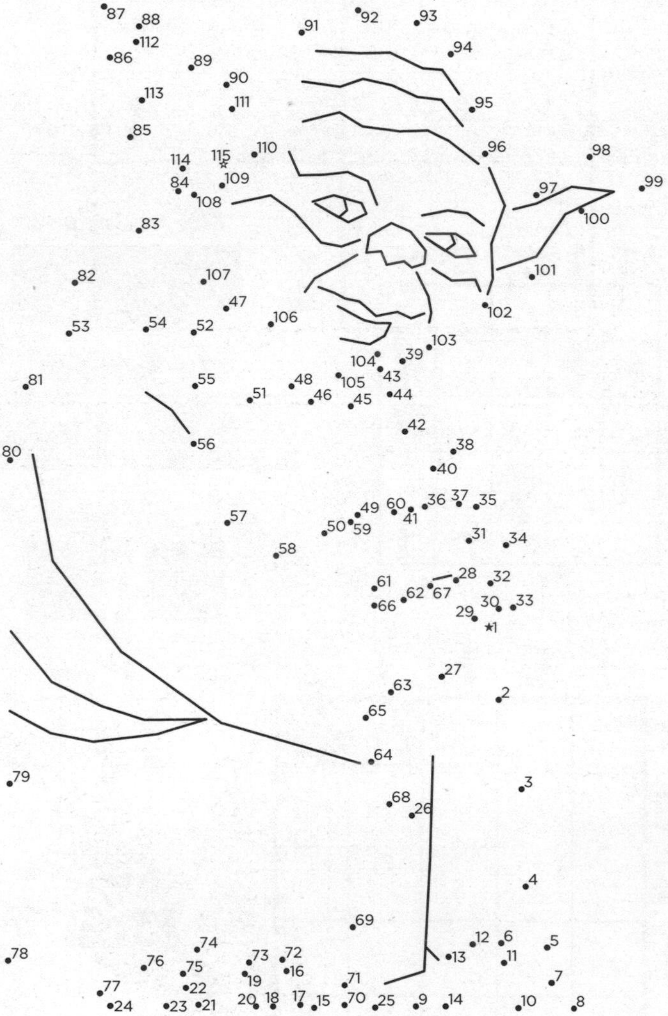

		I			
			I		A
K		A		N	
	E		K		I
E		N			
			G		

Kenobi's Keypad

DIFFICULTY:

The password for Obi-Wan Kenobi's secret lock-box has been encoded in the puzzle grid below. By solving the puzzle, you will reveal the password in the shaded squares, reading down and right from the top-left square.

To solve the puzzle, place the letters A, E, G, I, K and N once each in every row, column and bold-lined 3x2 box.

The Jedi Code

DIFFICULTY: 

Yoda has challenged Luke to crack an ancient Jedi cypher. Decode it, by replacing A with K, B with L, C with M and so on, using the cypher key below:

A	B	C	D	E	F	G	H	I	J	K	L	M	N	O	P	Q	R	S	T	U	V	W	X	Y	Z
K	L	M	N	O	P	Q	R	S	T	U	V	W	X	Y	Z	A	B	C	D	E	F	G	H	I	J

Fqjyudsu oek ckij xqlu,

____

co oekdw fqtqmqd - Oetq

____

Secret Sector

DIFFICULTY: 

Padmé Amidala is on a secret mission to meet a Republic spy, but the precise sector she needs to collect them from has been encoded within the grid below. The sector is five digits long, and written from left-to-right across the centre as marked by the grey bar – but first she needs to fill in the grid!

Place the numbers 1 to 5 once each into every row and column of the puzzle, and in such a way that two identical numbers never touch – not even diagonally.

	3		1	
2				3
3				5
	4		3	

Species Expertise

DIFFICULTY: 

Place all of the listed galactic species into the grid, once each, so that they read either across or down with one letter per box. Ignore any spaces or punctuation in the names of the species when writing them into the grid.

4 letter words
Bith
Ewok
Hutt
Jawa

5 letter words
Drall
Duros
Human

6 letter words
Cerean
Gungan
Yuzzum

7 letter words
Crolute
Ortolan
Wookiee

8 letter words
Aqualish
Besalisk
Ithorian
Pantoran

10 letter words
Dactillion
Neimoidian

11 letter word
Mon Calamari

Mystery Mosaic

DIFFICULTY: 

Colour in each of the numbered shapes to reveal a hidden image of a significant figure, leaving the unnumbered shapes empty.

Use the following colours:

1 = black; 2 = yellow; 3 = orange; 4 = red; 5 = brown

Clumsy Clean-up

DIFFICULTY: 

Jar Jar has knocked over a stack of storage containers, breaking four of them! Can you match the two halves of each one together? One remains intact, so you can tell what they should look like:

Podrace Pandemonium

DIFFICULTY: 

Greedo and Malakili are discussing the Boonta Eve Classic Podrace. The three podracers to cross the finish line were Sebulba, Dud Bolt and Gasgano.

Greedo says that Sebulba came first and Dud Bolt came second. Malakili says Gasgano came first and Sebulba came second. Neither of them are correct. Each of them has got one thing right and one thing wrong.

Who really came first, second and third?

1. ____________________________________

2. ____________________________________

3. ____________________________________

Be Crafty!

DIFFICULTY:

Find all of the listed vehicles in the word search grid. Their names can be written either forwards or backwards, and in any direction – including diagonally. Ignore any spaces or dashes when looking for the names.

T A R C A R G O S H I P D T K A
R R Y C X W I N G F I G H T E R
P O D R A C E R K H S F E E R O
R E B A E P E I S A R S I E R T
E C I I I L R N N I T A K T T C
Y E O I T S U D G A R I T R H I
O Y S T A G C A R E R O I N C D
R I U T D R T H H T C R E S A R
T H I I A E O S S T A E F C Y E
S N O W S P E E D E R B I X E T
E R L S P A I T K H S O G S C N
D E S E R T S K I F F I H A A I
R S R E K L A W T S T A T S P O
A T A T W A L K E R P S E A S K
T R A N S P O R T E R T R L P O
S T A R C R U I S E R O R D A S

AT-AT walker
AT-ST walker
Cargo ship
Desert skiff
Droid gunship
Frigate
Interdictor
Podracer
Sandcrawler
Short hauler
Shuttle
Snowspeeder
Space yacht
Star cruiser
Star Destroyer
Starhopper
TIE fighter
TIE striker
Transporter
X-wing fighter

Hyperdrive Havoc

DIFFICULTY:

The *Millennium Falcon*'s hyperdrive is malfunctioning, and only R2-D2 can fix it! Can you work out how to wire up the circuit shown below? All of the circled components need to be connected together using only horizontal and vertical lines - not diagonals. Lines can't cross over a component, and the number on a component shows exactly how many lines must connect into it. Once they are connected correctly, you should be able to trace a path from any component to any other component, just by following one or more lines.

Here's an example solution, to show how it works:

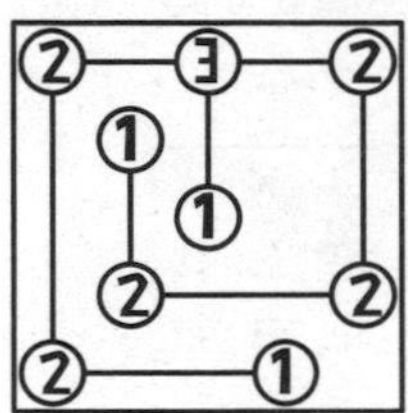

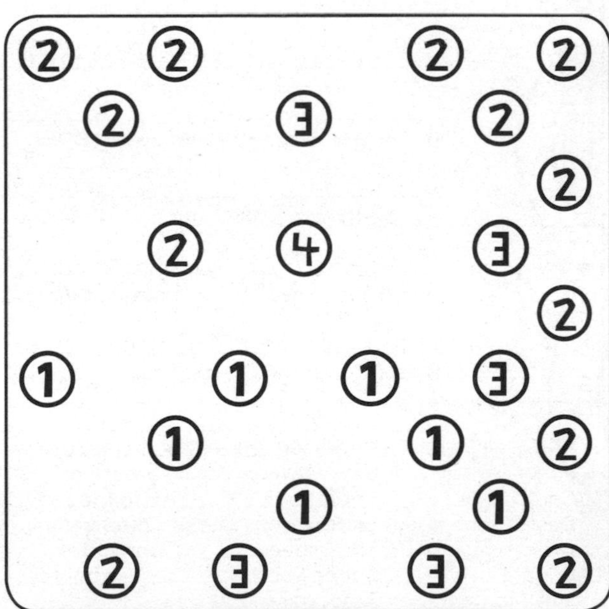

Rebel Riddle

DIFFICULTY: 

Han Solo needs your help to solve a mysterious riddle.
Can you work out what it means?

- My first is in **ARROW** and also in **CHEW**
- My second's in **COWER** but never in **CREW**
- My third is in **MOTOR** and also in **BOW**
- My fourth is in **EWOK** but never in **WOE**
- My fifth is in **X-WING** and also in **SIR**
- My sixth is in **REBEL** but never in **BLUR**
- My last is in **VADER** and also in **FOE**
- If you've found the answer, then write it below:

Chain Reaction

DIFFICULTY:

Rebel spies have recovered secret plans to the Death Star's reactor! Find a path from the thermal exhaust port to the core.

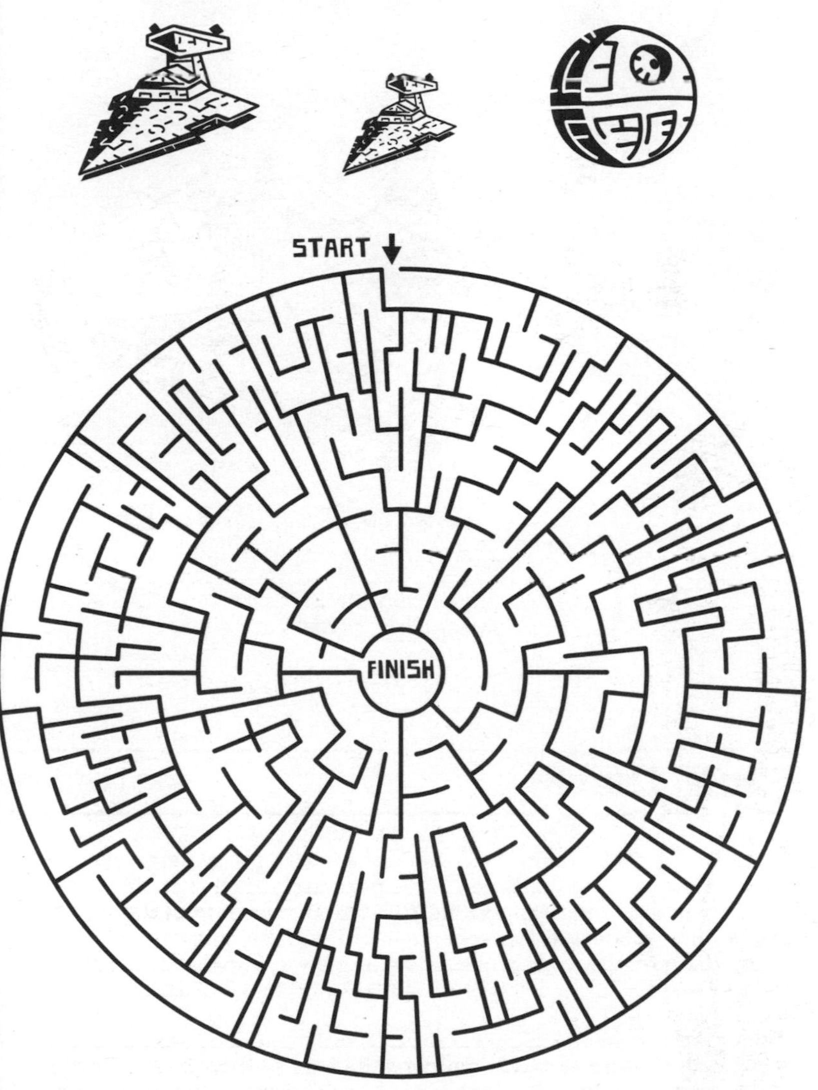

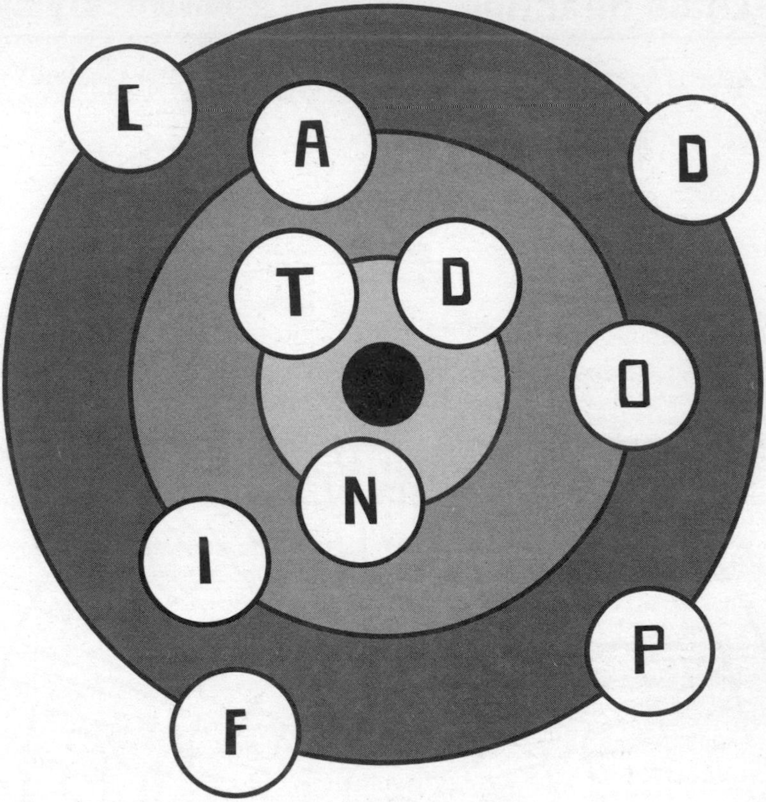

C

A

D

T

D

O

N

I

P

F

Spell Check

DIFFICULTY: 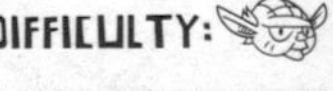

Qui-Gon is on a mission to a star system with ten planets, each identified by a unique letter. To be permitted to land on any of the three inner planets you must first land in turn on one of the four outer planets, followed by one of the three central planets. The route to any inner planet must also always spell out a three-letter word.

For example, you could spell out 'CAT' by landing on the 'C' in the outer ring, 'A' in the middle ring and 'T' in the inner ring.
There are more than 20 valid routes to the inner planets. How many can you find?

Cantina Conundrum

DIFFICULTY: 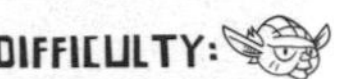

At Chalmun's Cantina on Tatooine the alien customers can get quite rowdy! Can you help seat them to prevent too much trouble? There are five Aqualish, five Bith, five Chagrians, five Devaronians, and five Eloms. You must make sure that the same type of alien is not seated more than once in any row or column, nor on any of the tables, marked with bold lines.

	A	B		
A			C	
B				D
	C			B
		E	B	

Musical Chairs

DIFFICULTY: 

Figrin D'an and the Modal Nodes have arrived at the Cantina, and all the customers are keen to catch the show – but you'll need to help rearrange the tables! Can you re-seat the aliens, as before making sure that there's only one of each species in each row, column and bold-lined table?

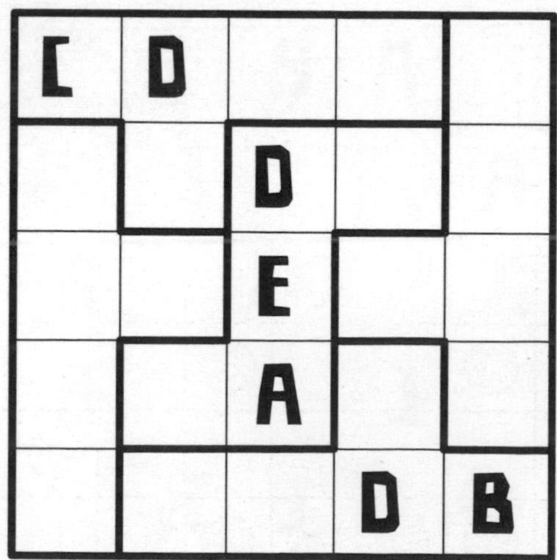

Mouse in a Maze

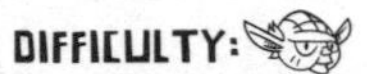

This MSE droid is lost in the Death Star's cargo hold! Only one of the following programs will allow it to leave without crashing into a storage pod. Which one should it follow? The direction of the arrow shows which way it is facing to begin with.

1. Rotate 90° right; forward 2 spaces, rotate 90° left; forward 3 spaces; rotate 90° left; forward 2 spaces; rotate 90° right; forward 3 spaces
2. Rotate 90° left; forward 1 space, rotate 90° right; forward 3 spaces; rotate 90° right; forward 1 space; rotate 90° left; forward 1 space; rotate 90° right; forward 1 space; rotate 90° left; forward 2 spaces
3. Forward 1 space; rotate 90° left; forward 1 space; rotate 90° right; forward 2 spaces; rotate 90° right; forward 1 space; rotate 90° left; forward 1 space; rotate 90° right; forward 2 spaces; rotate 90° left; forward 2 spaces

EXIT

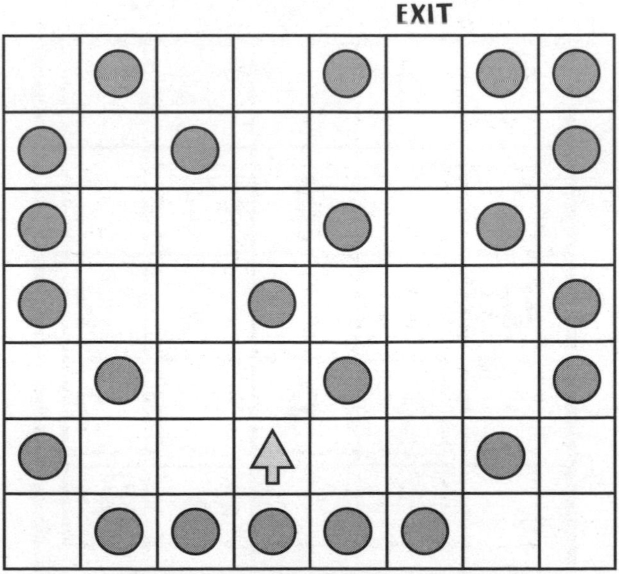

Maul Aboard!

DIFFICULTY:

Darth Maul is navigating a minefield in his Sith Interceptor. Some of the empty squares in the grid conceal deadly mines, and the numbers show how many of their touching squares – including diagonally touching squares – contain one. None of the numbered squares contain mines, and no square can contain more than one mine.

Can you find all of the mines?

	0			
		3	5	
0	1			2
	4	4		2
			2	

Repair Kit

DIFFICULTY:

Kit Fisto needs to repair an underwater reactor by reconnecting the power lines. By using the clues in the grid below, can you work out the exact path to trace? You start at number 1 and trace from 1 to 2, from 2 to 3, from 3 to 4 and so on all the way up until you reach number 25 – but the problem is that not all of the numbers are given, and it is up to you to work out where they all go. You also know that you only ever trace paths using horizontal and vertical lines – never diagonally.

Here's an example solution using 1 to 16, to show how it works:

	6		22	
4	7		23	24
		19		
2	9		13	16
	10		14	

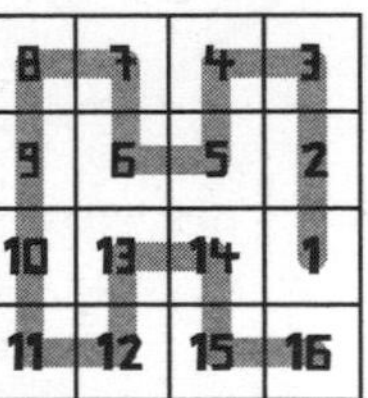

8	7	4	3
9	6	5	2
10	13	14	1
11	12	15	16

Calamari Code

DIFFICULTY:

Admiral Ackbar's password is a single nine-letter word. Can you dial it in, by using each letter exactly once to spell out the word?

Once you have found the nine-letter word, how many more words can you make using this dial? Each word should use the centre letter plus two or more of the other letters in any order. You can't use any of the letters more than once in a single word, however. There are at least 30 words to find.

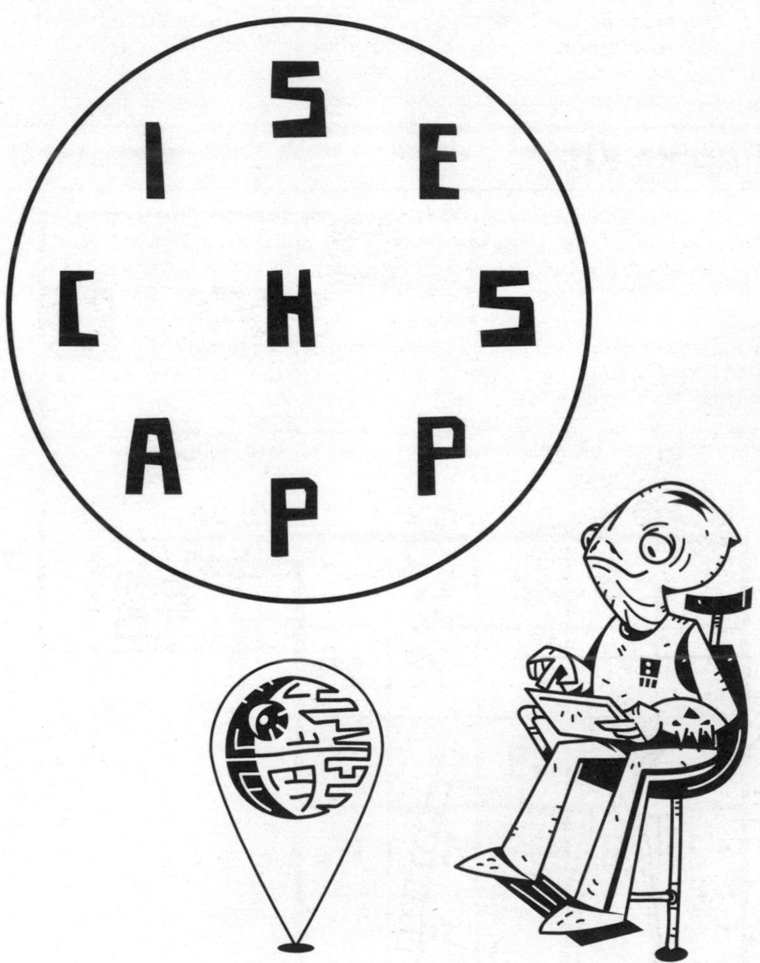

Eye Spy

DIFFICULTY: 

Cassian has intercepted coded plans to a secret enemy lab, revealing where all of its hidden security cameras are. He knows the following:

- Cameras are only found in empty squares, not the shaded squares, and only one in each square.
- Numbers in the shaded squares tell you how many camera there are in the squares immediately to the left, right, above or below.
- Cameras can see all the way left, right, up and down from their square, but not through shaded squares.
- No two cameras can see each other.
- All empty squares can be seen by at least one camera.

Can you work out where all of the cameras are? Two have been added to get you started.

	3				
		2	1		0
		0	0		
				1	

Boba's Blaster

DIFFICULTY:

Boba Fett is showing off his blaster skills at the practice range. He's such a good marksman, he can get any score he wants!

Help him prove it by hitting one number in the outer ring, one number in the centre ring, and one number in the innermost ring each time. These three numbers must add up to the right total. For example, to score '15' you would blast the 4 in the outer ring, the 8 in the centre ring, and the 3 in the inner ring, since 4 + 8 + 3 = 15.

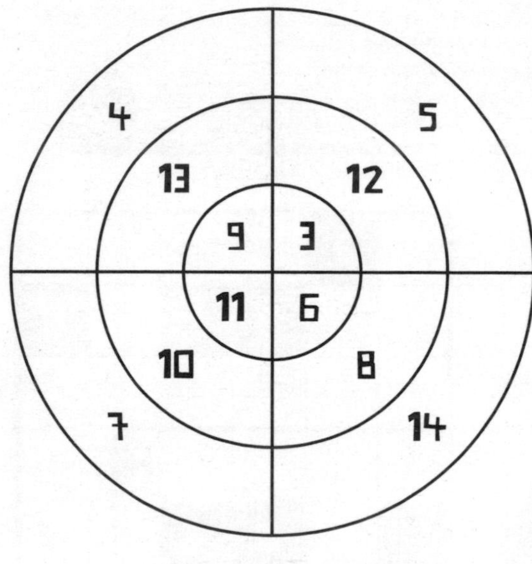

Scores to make:
16
32
36

Binary Brain

DIFFICULTY: 

Lobot keeps the computerised systems of Cloud City running using his cyborg brain! Can you help him fix this corrupted data file?

- Place four '0's and four '1's into each row and column
- There cannot be more than two '0's or two '1s' in sequence in any row or column

	0	0	1		0		1
0		1				0	1
0			1				0
	0	1		1			
			0		1	0	
1				0			0
0	1				0		1
1		0		0	1	0	

Rancor Rampage

DIFFICULTY:

Jabba's rancor pen is broken and the beast is running loose! Bring the force field back online by joining the force field posts together using only horizontal and vertical lines. Some parts of the force field are still working – draw the rest back in so that every post is used. The force field must form a single loop, without any crossing or touching parts.

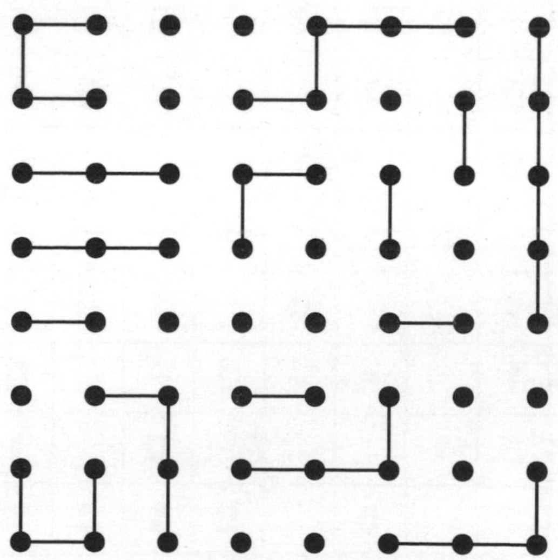

Just Jedi

DIFFICULTY:

The Jedi Council has seen many wise Masters, from Obi-Wan Kenobi and Mace Windu to Yoda and Qui-Gon Jinn. Can you fit all the listed names into the grid below?

6 letter word
Yaddle

7 letter words
Plo Koon
Shaak Ti

8 letter word
Eeth Koth

9 letter words
Adi Gallia
Even Piell

10 letter words
Ki-adi-mundi
Saesee Tiin
Stass Allie
Yarael Poof

11 letter words
Aayla Secura
Depa Billaba

12 letter word
Oppo Rancisis

13 letter word
Coleman Trebor

14 letter word
Luminara Unduli

Wookiee Wiring

DIFFICULTY:

Can you help Chewie fix the navicomputer? Connect all of the marked pairs of network ports. Draw a path between each pair of identical numbers, using only horizontal and vertical lines. To avoid data corruption, the paths cannot cross each other, and only one path can enter any square. Here's an example solution to show how it works:

1	2				3	4
				2		
		5				
	6		1			
			6		4	5
7					3	
		7				

Cutting Capers

DIFFICULTY: 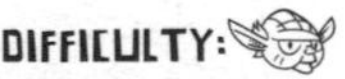

Lando is planning a heist. To gain access to a top-secret facility he needs four identical keys. Help him cut the keys from the piece of material shown below, cutting only along the grid lines. Each one of the four keys must be identical in shape, although they may appear rotated relative to one another - but not reflected. All of the material must be used, without any bits left over.

Can you work out where to cut?
Hint: there are 12 squares in the shape, so each key must consist of exactly 3 squares.

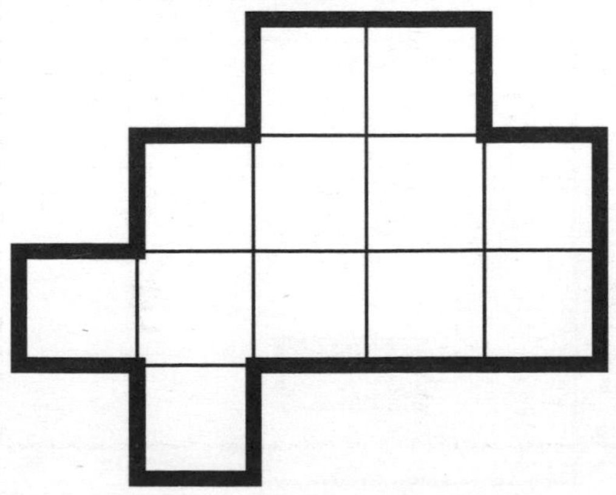

Bounty Hunt

DIFFICULTY:

The bounty hunter Zuckuss is tracking his latest target's movements. Only the start and end points of the target's route are now known, as shown by the black dots on the map below.

Work out the correct route by drawing a path from one black dot to the other, using horizontal and vertical lines to connect dots. The path cannot cross over any of the solid grey obstacles, and it cannot cross over or touch itself at any point. Numbers outside the grid show how many of the dots in each row and column that the loop visits.

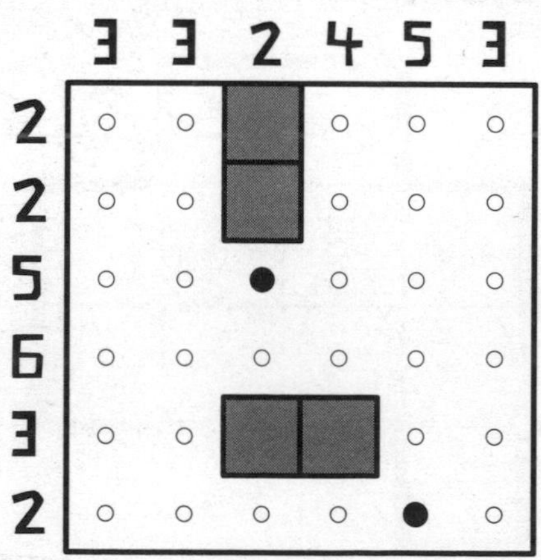

Symbol Search

DIFFICULTY: 

Dengar the bounty hunter is tracking his latest target. Each of his quarry's hideouts is marked on a map with a different symbol. To find where the target is hiding now, Dengar must work out what the last symbol will be . . . Can you crack the code?

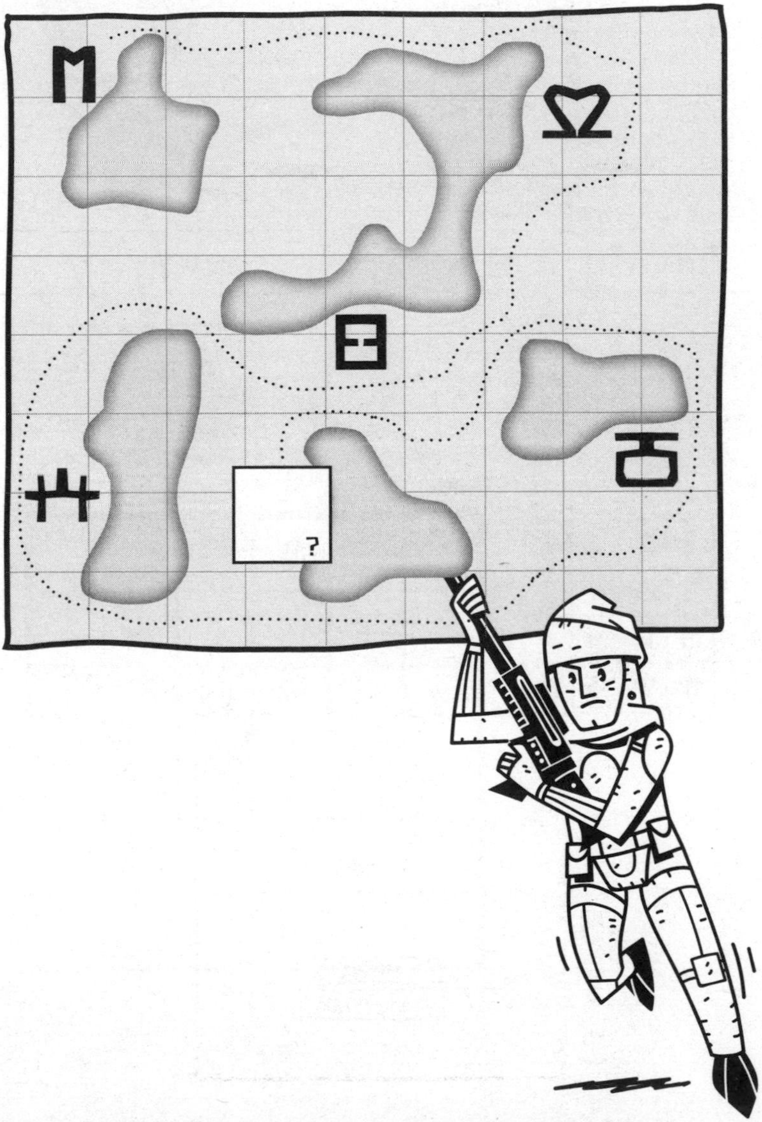

Leia Lines

DIFFICULTY: 

Princess Leia has been given the code to a secret rebel base. To open it, start at number 1 and trace from 1 to 2, from 2 to 3, from 3 to 4 and so on all the way up until you reach number 36 – but the problem is that not all of the numbers are given, and it is up to you to work out where they all go. You also know that you only ever trace paths using horizontal and vertical lines – never diagonally.

Here's an example solution using 1 to 16, to show how it works:

8	7	4	3
9	6	5	2
10	13	14	1
11	12	15	16

		9	10		
	1			14	
5		7	12		18
34		32	25		19
	30			23	
		28	27		

Crop Rotation

DIFFICULTY: 

Aunt Beru waters her plants every morning, visiting every empty square exactly once each in a loop. She only travels horizontally or vertically between squares, not diagonally, and the loop does not cross over or touch itself at any point. Can you trace her route? Here is an example:

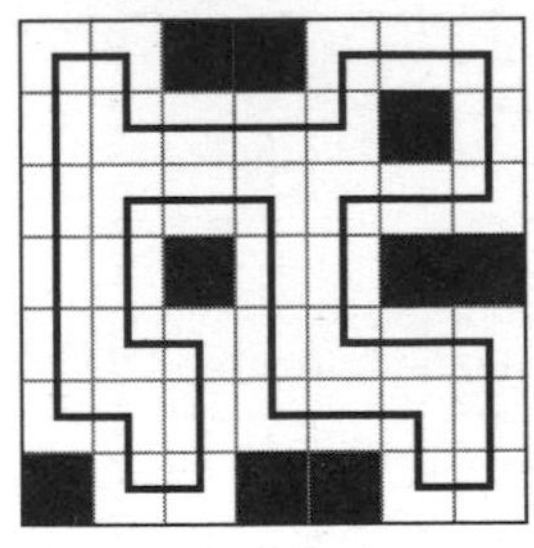

Riddle of the Sands

DIFFICULTY:

Tusken Raiders ride their banthas single-file, to hide their numbers, but with your Jedi techniques you can find out some things . . . Some Tusken Raiders and banthas passed this way recently; there were twenty-two creatures in all, and between them they had seventy-two legs.

Tusken Raiders have two legs, banthas have four legs. How many Tusken Raiders were there, and how many banthas?

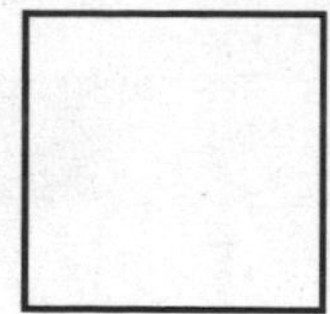

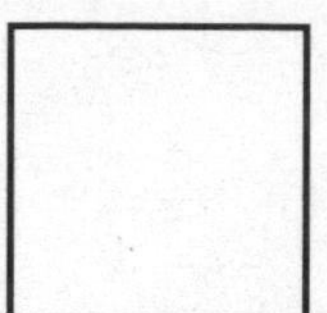

Mixed Messages

DIFFICULTY:

Yoda has left a secret message for Luke Skywalker. Can you work out what it says? Think back . . .

Od ro od ton - ereht si on yrt

____

____

Puzzle Protocol

DIFFICULTY:

Join the numbered dots in numerical order from 1 to 123 to reveal a well-known protocol droid.

Cryptic Crumb

DIFFICULTY:

Salacious Crumb has played a prank on the staff at Jabba's Palace – he's turned all the signs into puzzles! Can you work out what is kept in the room with the sign below?

Numbers at the start of a row or column indicate the number of shaded squares in that row or column. All shaded squares within a row or column touch each other in a continuous line, without any unshaded squares between them. Some squares have been shaded to start you off.

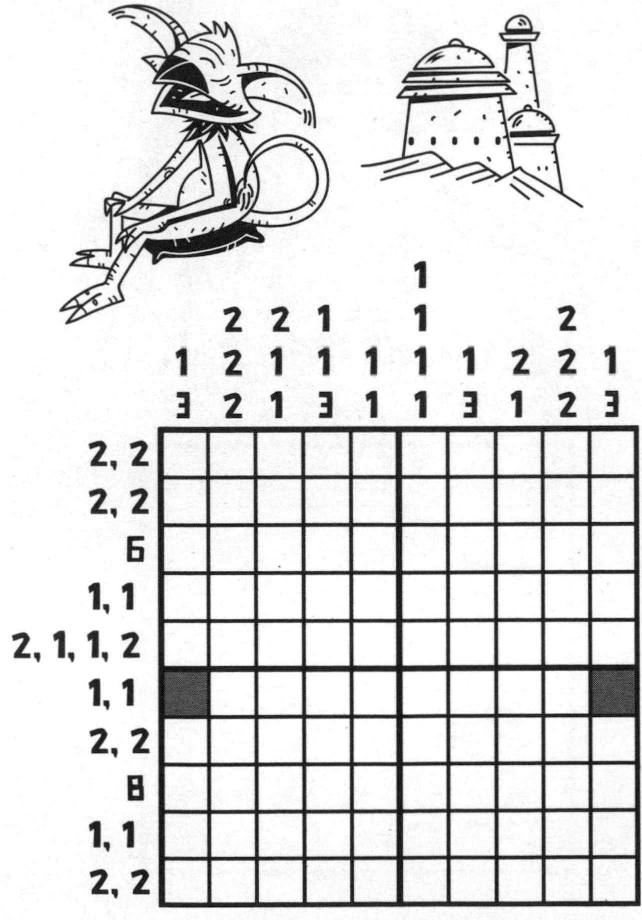

Turbolaser Trouble

DIFFICULTY:

Red Leader is starting his attack run! Each of the circles in the map below represents a turbolaser, and each laser guards an area that is a perfect square. Divide the map up into squares of various sizes by drawing along the grid lines, so that each turbolaser is in exactly one square, and all of the map is covered. Two squares have been added to get you started.

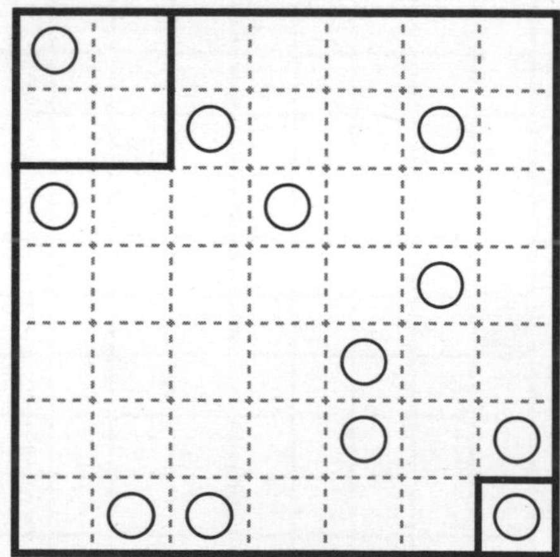

Porkins Peril

DIFFICULTY:

It's Porkins' turn to pilot his X-wing through the turbolaser barrage! Divide the map up into squares of various sizes by drawing along the grid lines, so that each turbolaser is in exactly one square, and all of the map is covered by squares.

Biggs Baffler

DIFFICULTY:

Biggs Darklighter needs to rendezvous with the rebel fleet, but the precise sector has been encoded within the grid below. The sector is six digits long, and written from left-to-right across the grid as shown by the grey bar – but first you need to fill in the grid!

Place the numbers 1 to 6 once each into every row and column of the puzzle, and in such a way that two identical numbers never touch – not even diagonally.

1		2	6		4
3					1
5					6
4		3	2		5

Power Pack

DIFFICULTY:

This power droid needs to recharge a stack of batteries. Each battery in the stack needs to be charged to a level equal to the sum of the two batteries immediately below it - just like the stack to the left. Using this knowledge, complete all of the missing numbers so that you know exactly how much charge needs to go in each battery.

Dark Path

DIFFICULTY:

Emperor Palpatine knows that FEAR leads to HATE. Try to change FEAR to HATE in eight steps. At each step you should change just one letter to make a new word, without rearranging any of the letters. For example, you *could* start by changing FEAR to BEAR, though that will lead you down the wrong path . . .

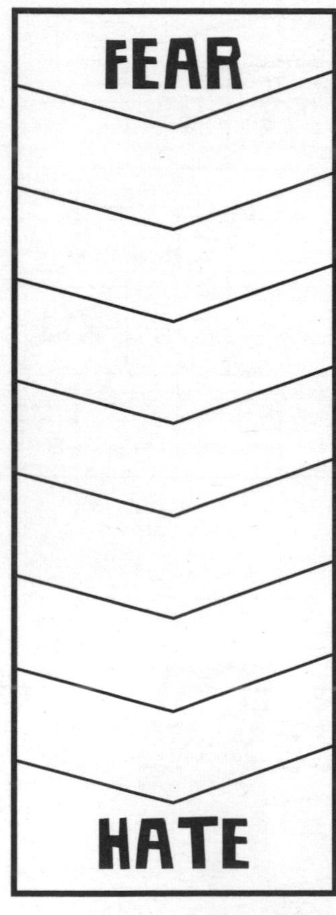

Force Fix

DIFFICULTY: 

Anakin's ship the *Twilight* has broken down and his Padawan Ahsoka is trying to fix it. Can you see how to wire up the circuit shown below? All of the circled components need to be connected together using only horizontal and vertical lines. Lines can't cross over a component, and the number on a component shows exactly how many lines must connect into it. Once they are connected correctly, you should be able to trace a path from any component to any other component, just by following one or more lines.

Here's an example solution, to show how it works:

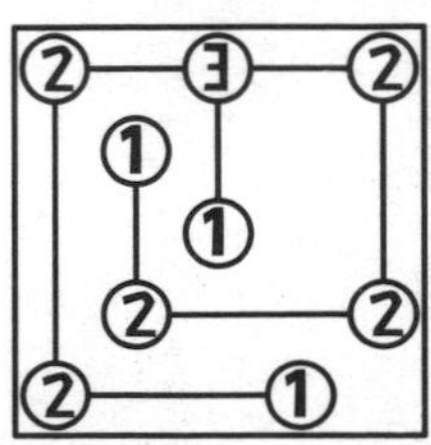

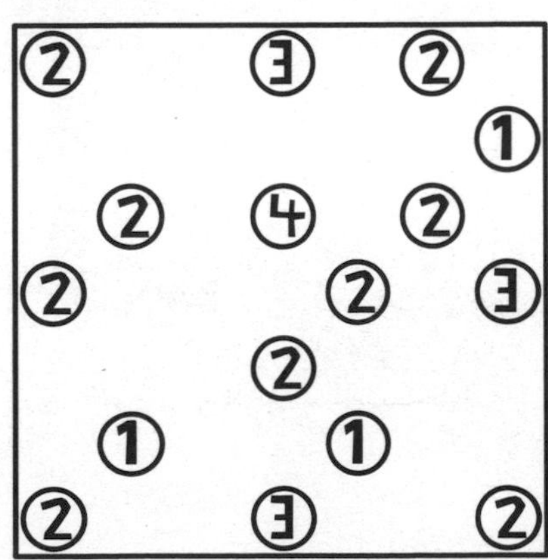

Solutions

Who's Who?

pg. 6

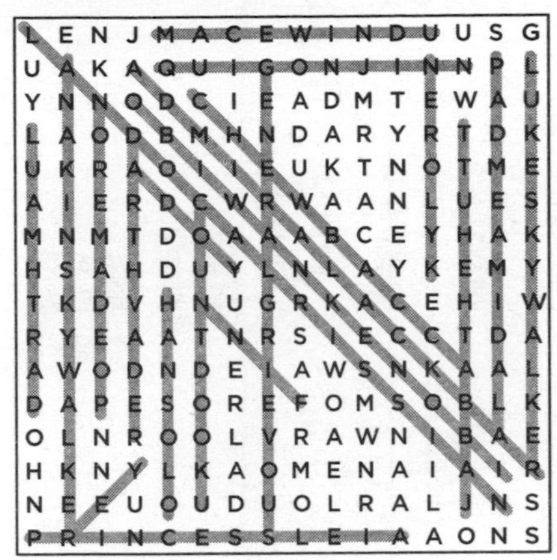

Binary Baffler

pg. 7

0	0	1	0	1	1
0	1	0	1	1	0
1	0	1	0	0	1
0	0	1	0	1	1
1	1	0	1	0	0
1	1	0	1	0	0

Transmission Impossible

pg. 8

RESULT 43	RESULT 51	RESULT 8	RESULT 32
+20	×3	÷6	+20
÷3	+6	+6	÷4
-11	÷4	×2	×12
+10	×11	-10	÷2
×10	÷7	+17	-6
7	28	14	14

Traffic Jam

pg. 9

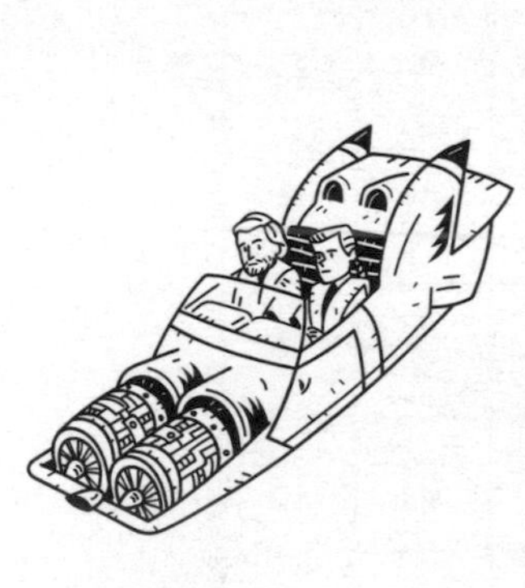

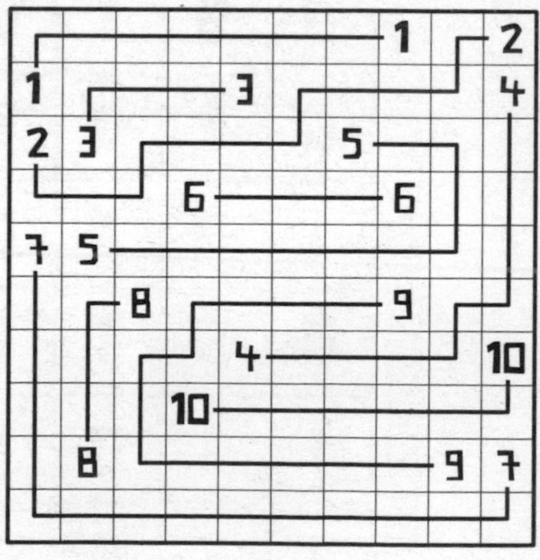

Boushh Bewildered

pg. 10

The nine-letter word is **STARLIGHT**. Other words that can be spelt are: GIST, LIGHT, LIST, RATS, SIGH, SIGHT, STAR, TAR, TARS (plus RAT, as given in the example).

Puzzle Protocol

pg. 11

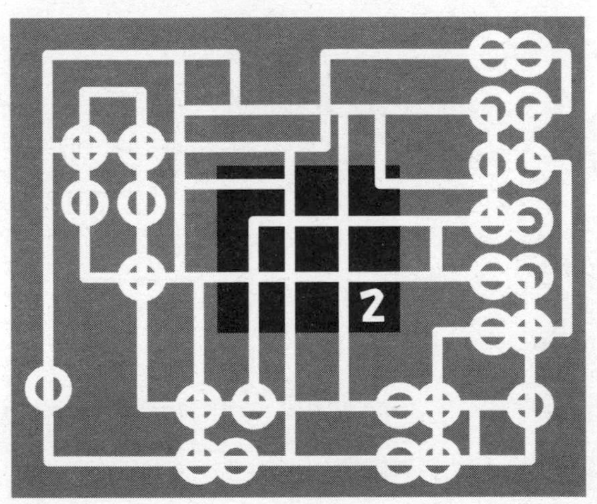

Greedy Greedo

pg. 12

1. CHEAT
2. STEEL
3. GRAND
4. GREED
5. STEAL
6. CRIED

Some other words that can be made with the sliders;

CHANT
GREAT
GREET
GRIND
SHEET
STEED
STINT

Corridor Code

pg. 13

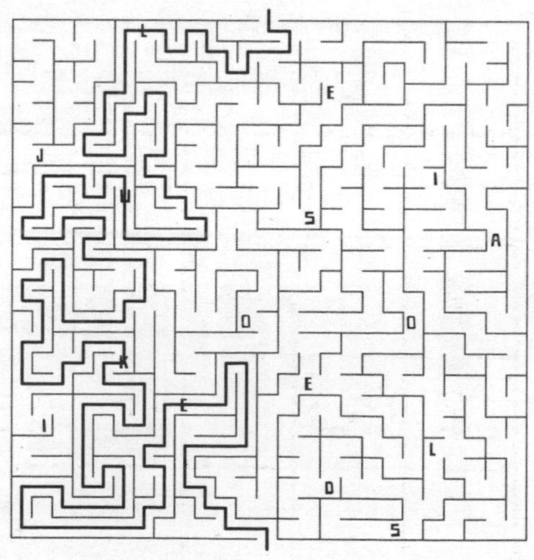

Mind Connection

pg. 14

MIND
MEND
SEND
SEED
SEES

Asteroid Field

pg. 15

	0		0	
1			2	2
2	asteroid	4	asteroid	asteroid
2	asteroid		asteroid	asteroid
			2	2

Jawa Junk

pg. 16

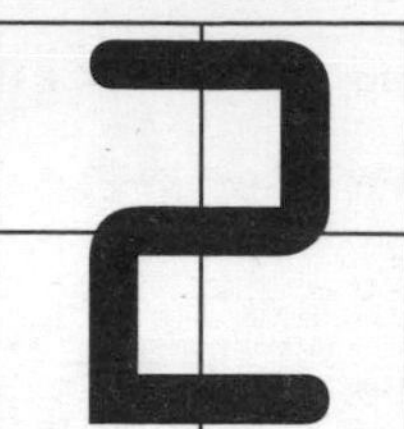

Guards, Guards!

pg. 17

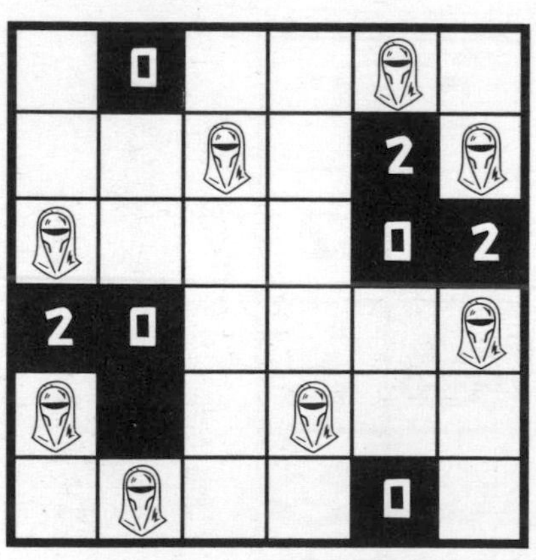

Cargo Conundrum

pg. 18

Ship 1: 15 = 4 + 11

Ship 2: 22 = 4 + 7 + 11

Ship 3: 26 = 5 + 9 + 12

Ship 4: 29 = 4 + 5 + 9 + 11

Ship 5: 34 = 4 + 7 + 11 + 12

Sign Language

pg. 19

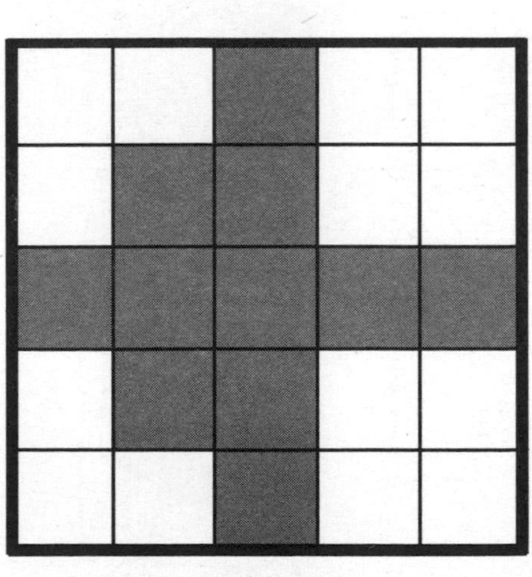

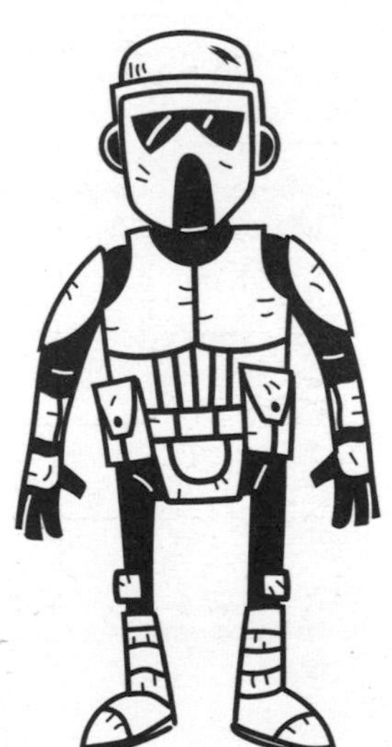

Rebel Run

pg. 20

Tarkin's Teaser

pg. 21

1. 27 – each number is equal to the previous number plus 4
2. 64 – each number is equal to the previous number times 2
3. 29 – the sequence is +2, +3, +4, +5, +6, +7 and so on
4. 47 – each number is equal to the previous two numbers added together
5. 3 – each number is equal to the previous number divided by 2

Hungry Hungry Hutt

pg. 22

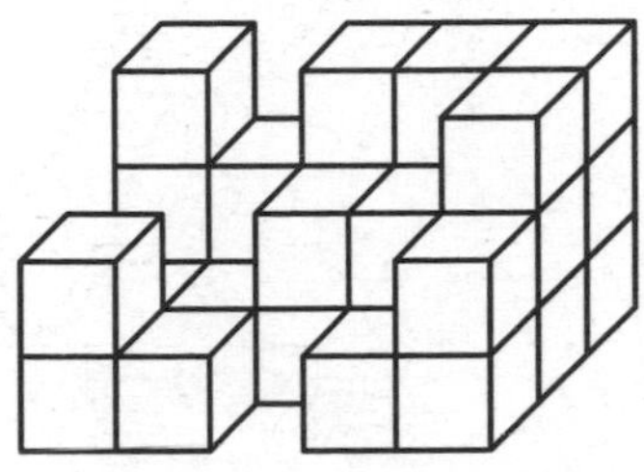

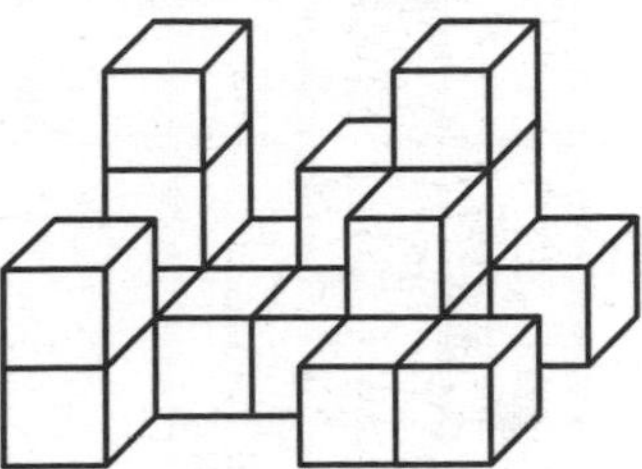

Left-hand pile: 29 fuel pods, consisting of 5 on the top layer, 10 on the middle layer and 14 on the bottom layer

Right-hand pile: 19 fuel pods, consisting of 2 on the top layer, 5 on the middle layer and 12 on the bottom layer

Star Tours

pg. 23

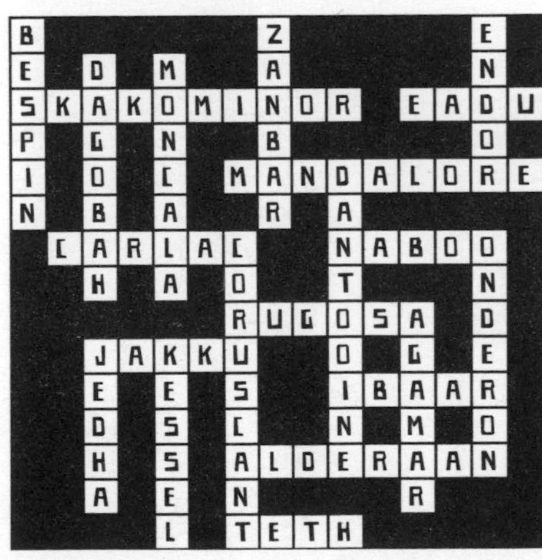

Lightsaber Lesson

pg. 24

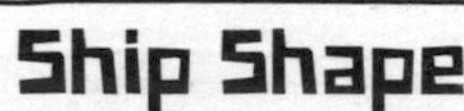

Ship Shape

pg. 25

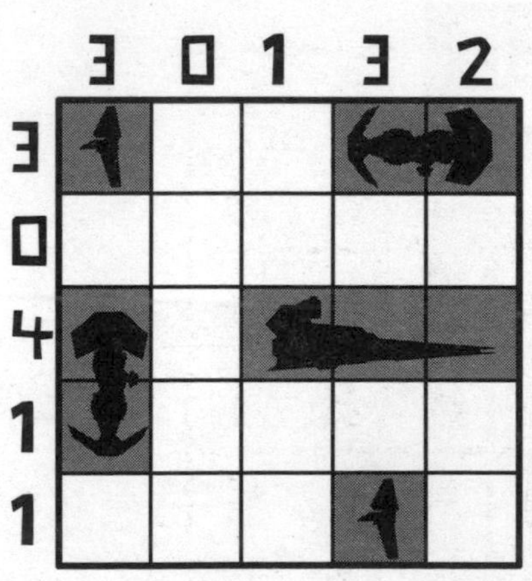

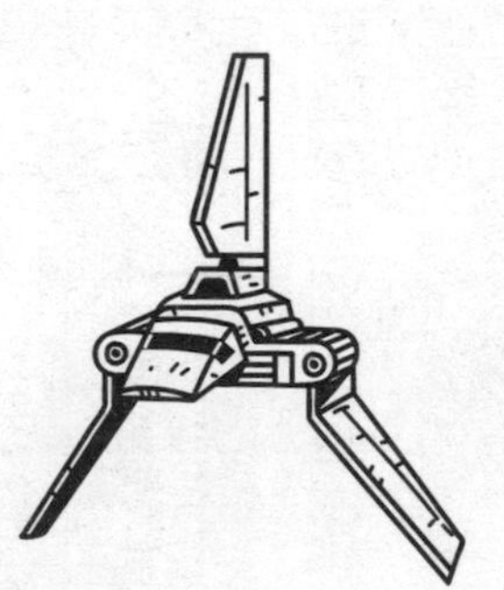

Mystery Master

pg. 26

Kenobi's Keypad

pg. 27

A	K	I	N	G	E
G	N	E	I	K	A
K	I	A	E	N	G
N	E	G	K	A	I
E	G	N	A	I	K
I	A	K	G	E	N

The Jedi Code

pg. 28

Patience you must have, my young Padawan - Yoda

Secret Sector

pg. 29

5	3	2	1	4
2	1	4	5	3
4	5	3	2	1
3	2	1	4	5
1	4	5	3	2

Species Expertise

pg. 30

		M	O	N	C	A	L	A	M	A	R	I		
			R		E									H
P	A	N	T	O	R	A	N							U
			O		E				Y	U	Z	Z	U	M
			L		A									A
J	A	W	A		N	E	I	M	O	I	D	I	A	N
			N				T				A			
		G		B	I	T	H		C		C		D	
		U		E			O		R		T		U	
		N		S			R		O		I		R	
		G		A			I		L		L		O	
D	R	A	L	L			A	Q	U	A	L	I	S	H
		N		I			N		T		I			U
				S					E	W	O	K		T
	W	O	O	K	I	E	E				N			T

Clumsy Clean-up

pg. 32

Podrace Pandemonium

pg. 33

If Greedo is right about Sebulba coming first, then he must be wrong about Dud Bolt coming second, and so the real order would be 1. Sebulba, 2. Gasgano, 3. Dud Bolt.

If Greedo is wrong about Sebulba coming first, then he must be right about Dud Bolt coming second, and so the real order would be 1. Gasgano, 2. Dud Bolt, 3. Sebulba.

If Malakili is right about Gasgano coming first, then he must be wrong about Sebulba coming second, and so the real order would be 1. Gasgano, 2. Dud Bolt, 3. Sebulba

If Malakili is wrong about Gasgano coming first, then he must be right about Sebulba coming second, and so the real order would be 1. Dud Bolt, 2. Sebulba, 3. Gasgano.

The answer must be the two orders that agree: 1. Gasgano, 2. Dud Bolt, 3. Sebulba.

Be Crafty!

pg. 34

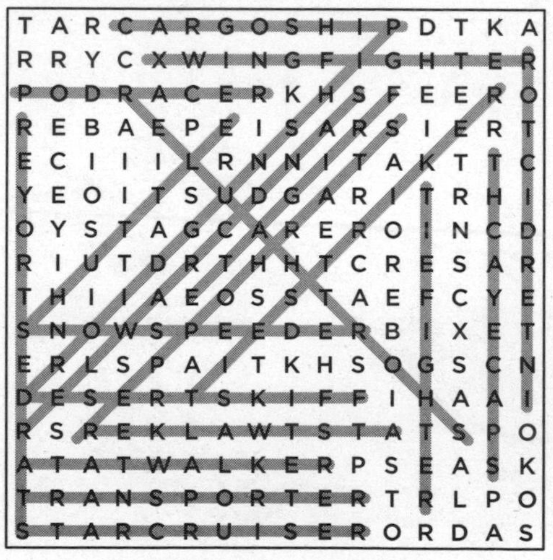

Hyperdrive Havoc

pg. 35

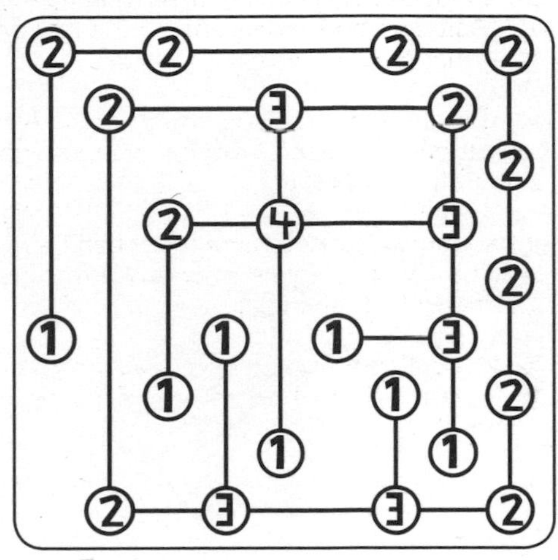

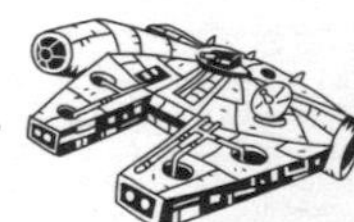

Rebel Riddle

pg. 36

The answer is:
WOOKIEE

Chain Reaction

pg. 37

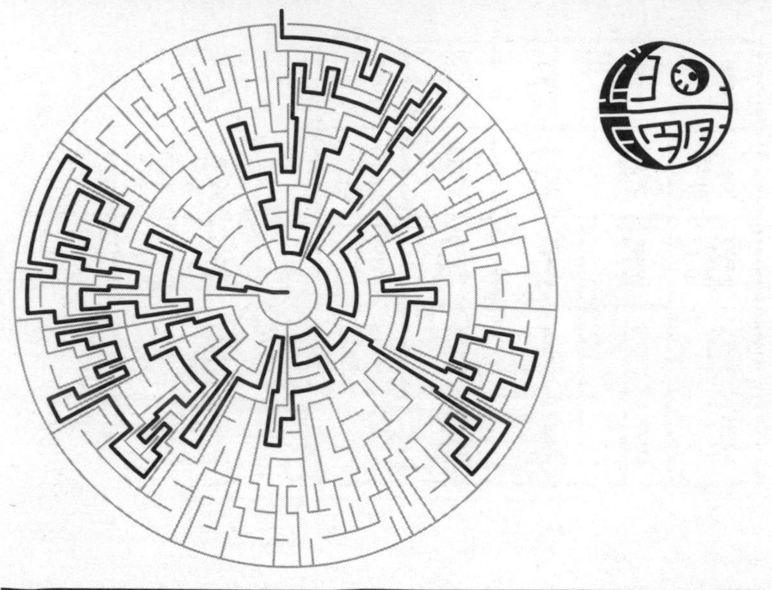

Spell Check

pg. 38

The following words can be made:

CAD	DAD	FAD	PAN
CAN	DAN	FAN	PAT
CAT	DID	FAT	PIN
COD	DIN	FIN	PIT
CON	DON	FIT	POD
COT	DOT	PAD	POT

These very unusual words can also be made:

DIT – another word for a 'dot' in Morse code
FID – a type of bar on a sailing ship

Cantina Conundrum

pg. 39

E	A	B	D	C
A	B	D	C	E
B	E	C	A	D
D	C	A	E	B
C	D	E	B	A

Musical Chairs

pg. 40

C	D	B	A	E
B	E	D	C	A
A	C	E	B	D
D	B	A	E	C
E	A	C	D	B

Mouse in a Maze

pg. 41

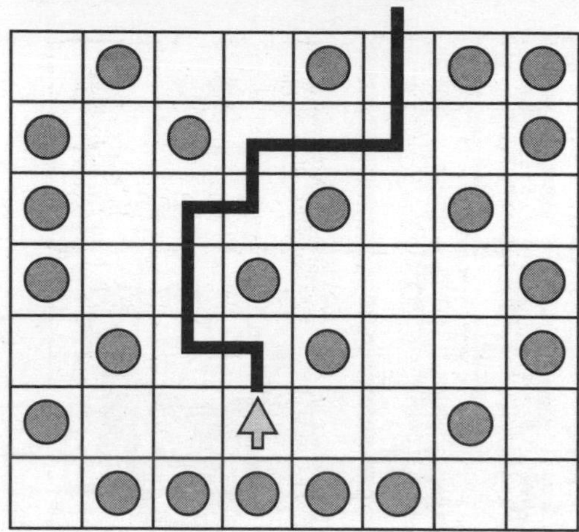

Program 3

Maul Aboard!

pg. 42

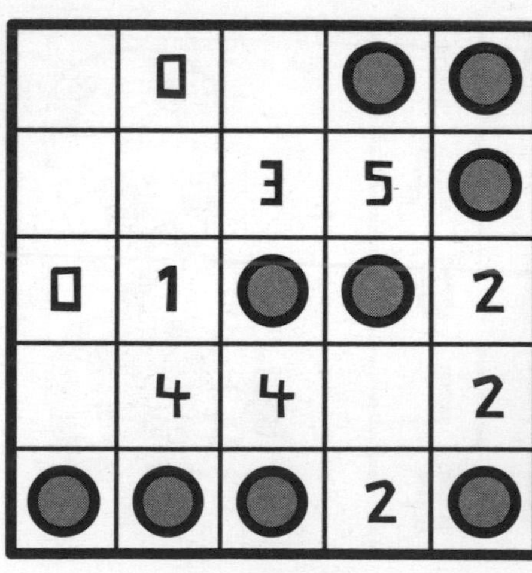

Repair Kit

pg. 43

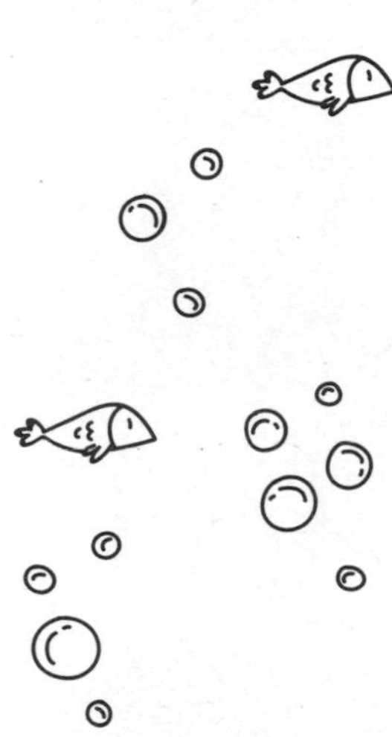

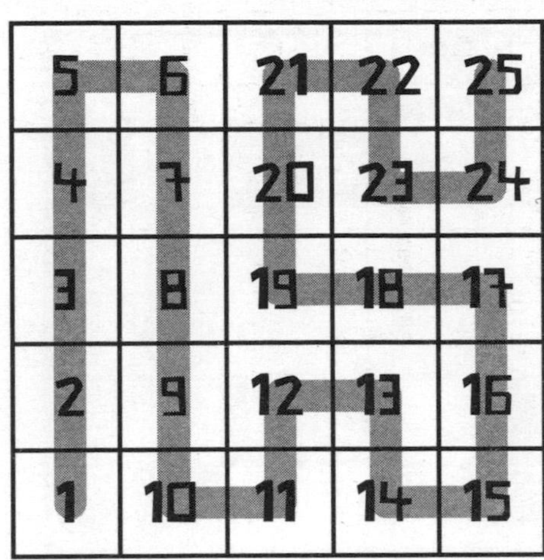

Calamari Code

pg. 44

The nine-letter word is **spaceship**.

Other words include ache, aches, ash, ashes, cash, cashes, chaise, chaises, chap, chaps, chase, chases, cheap, chess, chi, chip, chips, each, has, hasp, hasps, heap, heaps, hip, hips, his, hiss, peach, phase, phases, sash, shape, shapes, she, shies, ship and ships.

Eye Spy

pg. 45

Boba's Blaster

pg. 46

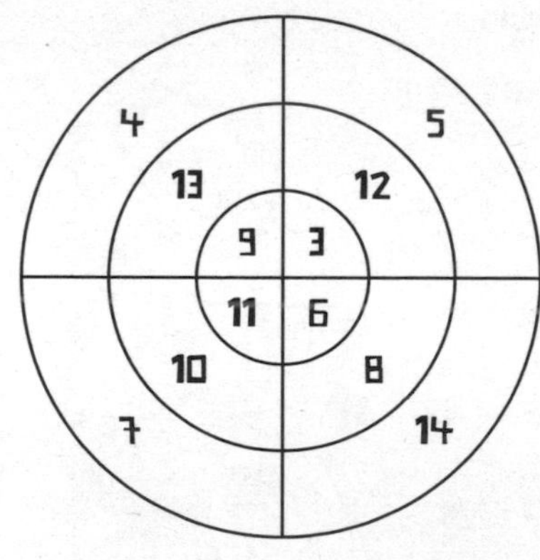

Scores to make:
16 = 5 + 8 + 3
32 = 14 + 12 + 6
36 = 14 + 13 + 9

Binary Brain

pg. 47

1	0	0	1	0	0	1	1
0	0	1	0	1	1	0	1
0	1	0	1	0	1	1	0
1	0	1	0	1	0	1	0
0	1	0	0	1	1	0	1
1	0	1	1	0	0	1	0
0	1	1	0	1	0	0	1
1	1	0	1	0	1	0	0

Rancor Rampage

pg. 48

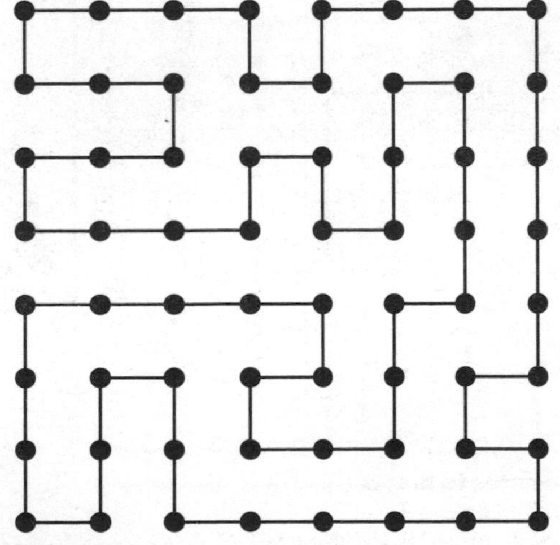

Just Jedi

pg. 49

			K				E	E	T	H	K	O	T	H		
			I				V									
		S	A	E	S	E	E	T	I	I	N					
			D				N									
			I		O	P	P	O	R	A	N	C	I	S	I	S
	Y		M				I									T
	A		U			D	E	P	A	B	I	L	L	A	B	A
	R		N				L		A					D		S
Y	A	D	D	L	E		L		Y					I		S
	E		I						L					G		A
	L				S				A		P			A		L
	P				H				S		L			L		L
C	O	L	E	M	A	N	T	R	E	B	O	R		L		I
	O				A				C		K			I		E
	F				K				U		O			A		
					T				R		O					
		L	U	M	I	N	A	R	A	U	N	D	U	L	I	

Wookiee Wiring

pg. 50

Cutting Capers

pg. 51

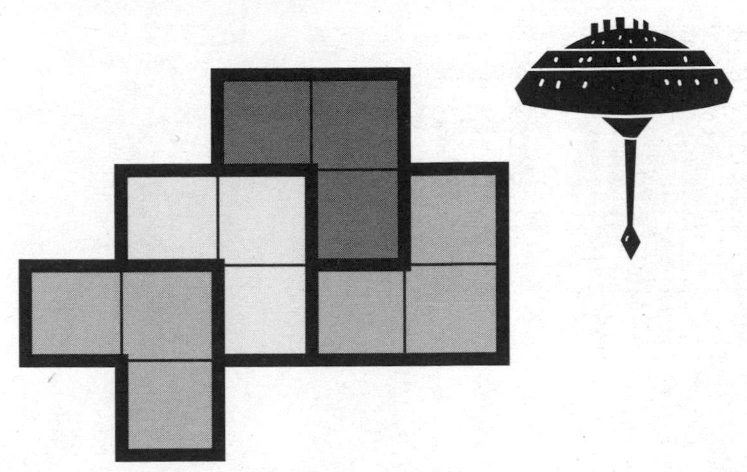

Bounty Hunt

pg. 52

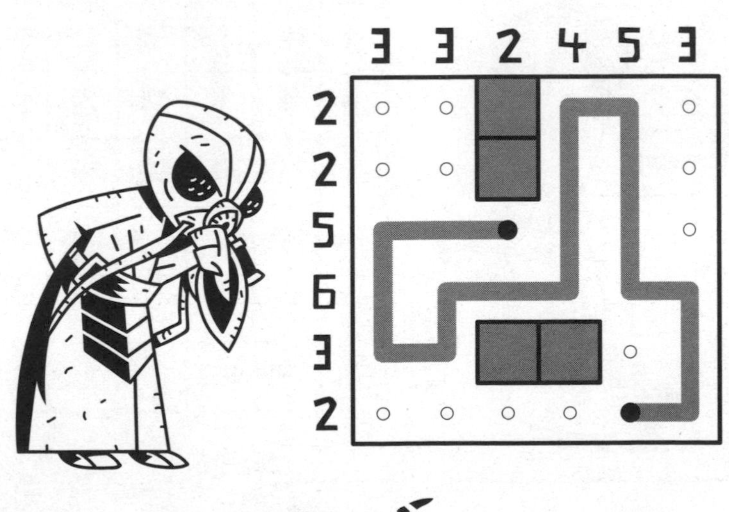

SYMBOL SEARCH

pg. 53

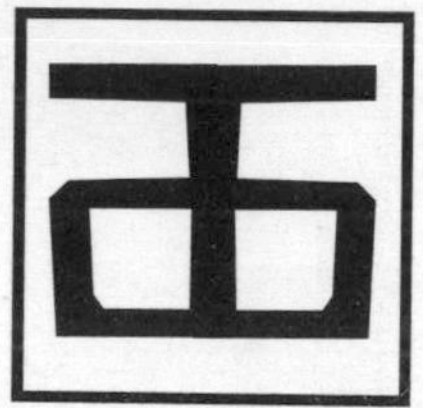

Leia Lines

pg. 54

3	2	9	10	15	16
4	1	8	11	14	17
5	6	7	12	13	18
34	33	32	25	24	19
35	30	31	26	23	20
36	29	28	27	22	21

Crop Rotation

pg. 55

Riddle of the Sands

pg. 56

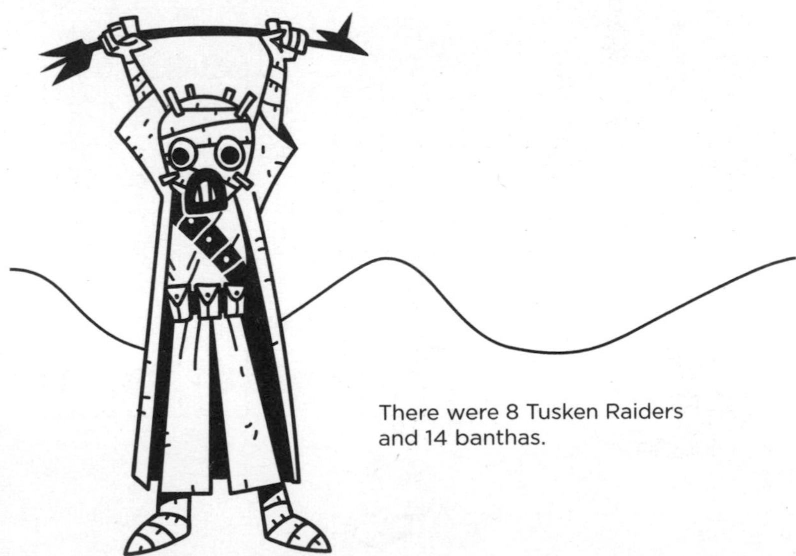

There were 8 Tusken Raiders and 14 banthas.

Mixed Messages

pg. 57

Do or do not - there is no try

Puzzle Protocol

pg. 58

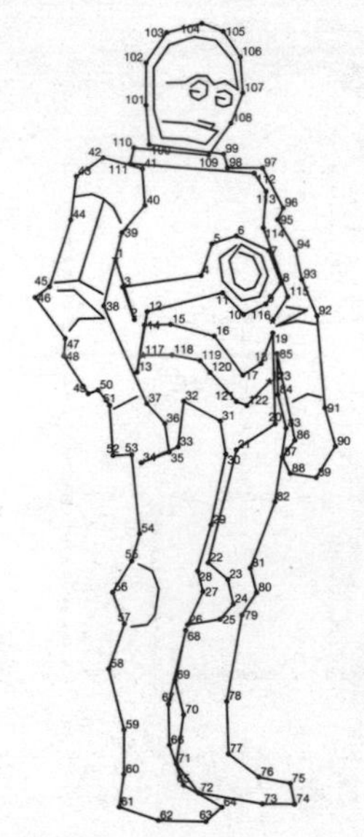

Cryptic Crumb

pg. 59

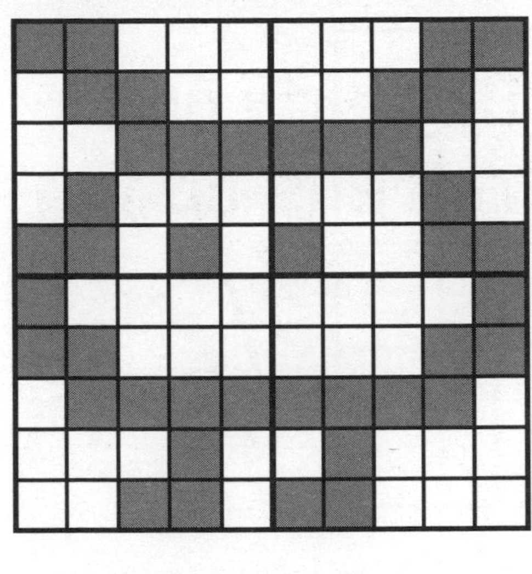

Turbolaser Trouble

pg. 60

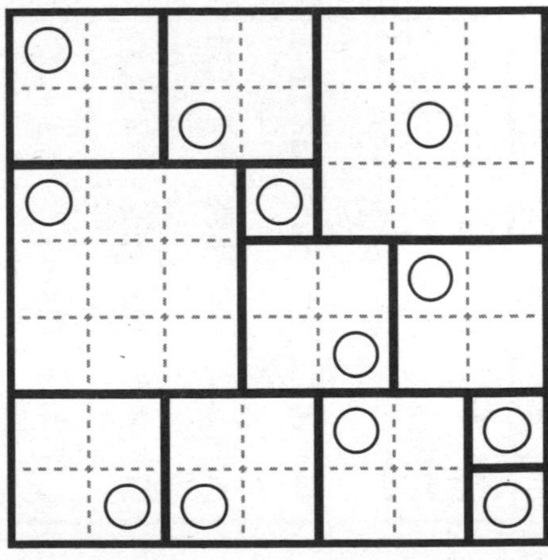

Porkins Peril

pg. 61

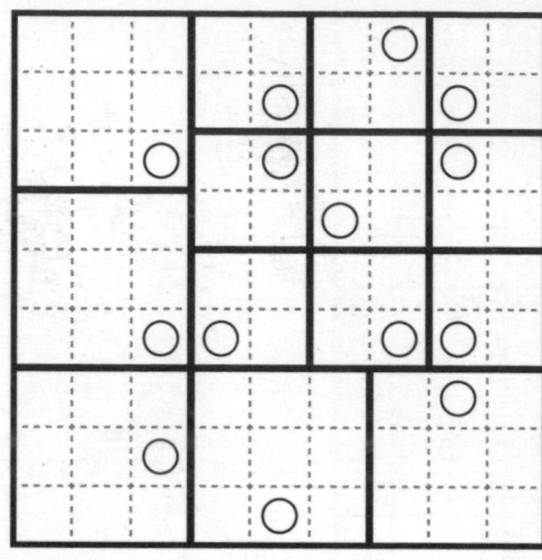

Biggs Baffler

pg. 62

1	3	2	6	5	4
6	5	4	1	3	2
3	2	6	5	4	1
5	4	1	3	2	6
2	6	5	4	1	3
4	1	3	2	6	5

Power Pack

pg. 63

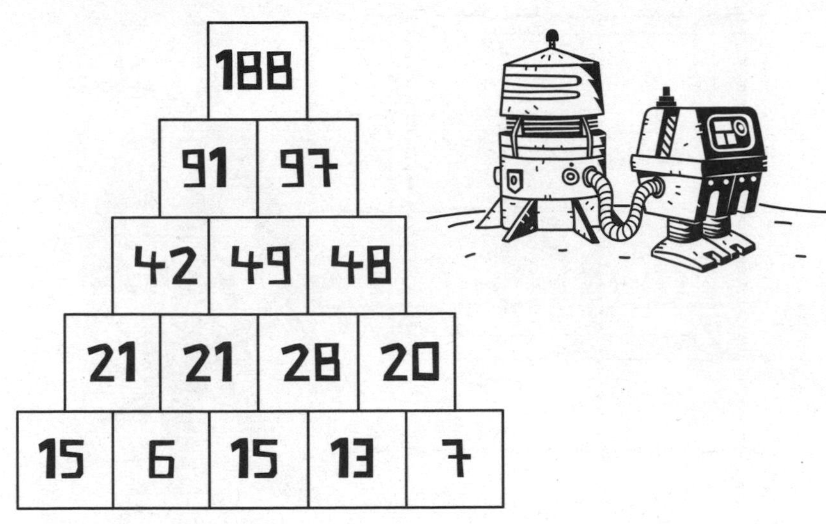

Dark Path

pg. 64

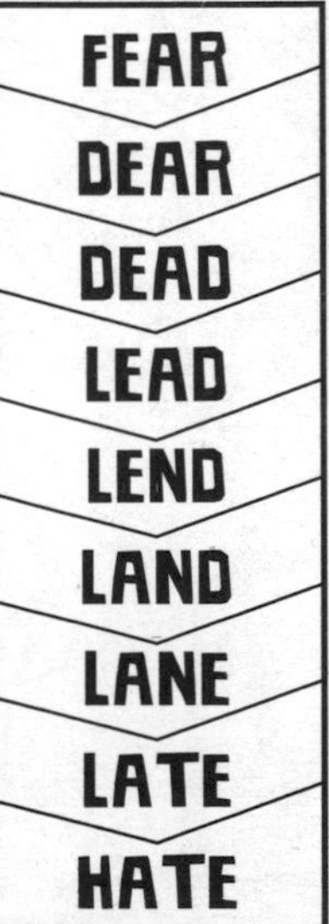

Force Fix

pg. 65

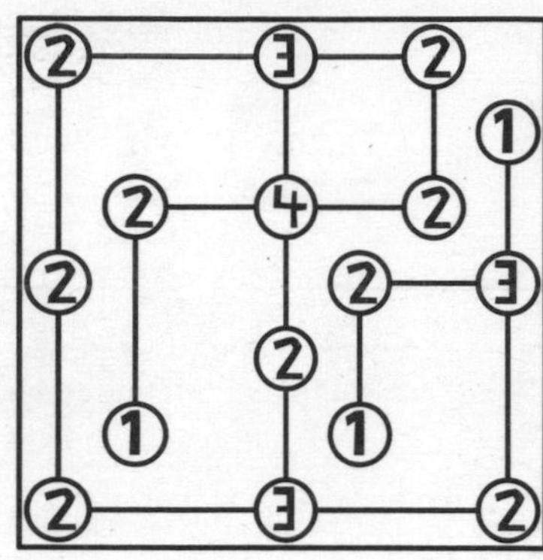

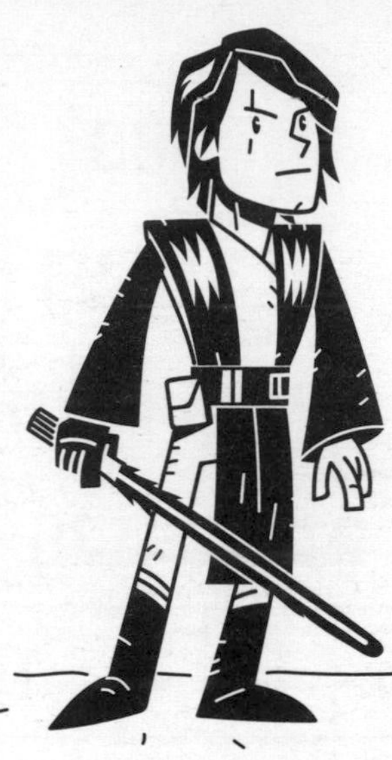

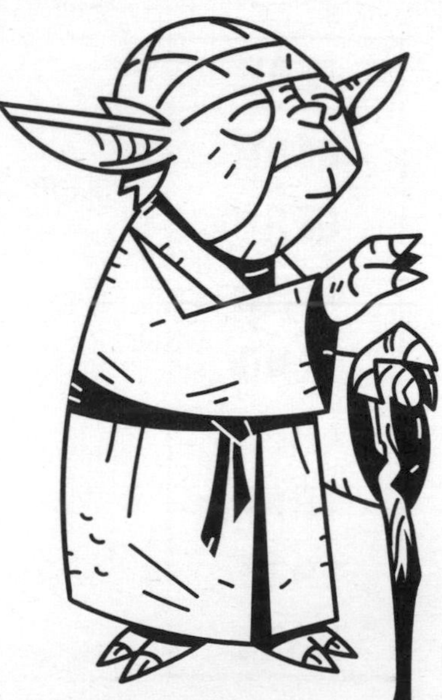
May the force be with you!